Rain Dance

RAIN DANCE

an
anthology

Published by Afritondo Media and Publishing 2022

First published in Great Britain in 2022
by Afritondo Media and Publishing
Preston, United Kingdom
www.afritondo.com

ISBN: 9781838027964

For all those who believe

CONTENTS

A child who is carried on the back has no idea how far the journey is.

African proverb

ON THE ROAD TO BYZANTIUM
Okwubi Godwin Adah

And therefore I have sailed the seas and come,
To the holy city of Byzantium.
W.B Yeats.

The woman and the child walk on the road as the sun trails behind them, leaving the sky a reddish hue, a sad, depressing colour, the colour of dying light. She leads the boy by the hand as they wade through smoke, dust, debris, and acridity. Behind them is nothing but waste, gnarled trees, and polluted land. Before them is more of the same, emptiness and death. In their world, few things move, and the things that do move are out to get you.

In the deathly silence, the woman hears the boy mutter to himself, gibberish she can't make sense of. She turns to question him, but the bang of a gunshot rends the air. Both woman and child stop, their bare feet biting into the earth, their eyes searching, their apprehension as thick as dust. It is almost dark, and they need a place to pass the night, a place to rest and hide from other things that move. The child has become restless and is still muttering to himself, so she asks, 'What is it?'

'Nothing,' he says.

She fixes him a hard stare, and he answers, 'I was singing.'

She knows he is lying, but she lets it go. She tucks anything else she wants to say underneath her tongue and faces forward. Her eyes skim over the bleak backdrop before her as she searches for shelter. The town is littered with burnt houses and sleeping cars, presenting an ugly façade that dominates every street and corner. The land is dead and parched as the sun rules with an iron fist, beating anything unlucky enough to still be alive into submission. The road still stretches on, cutting through the empty town. Some buildings still stand, tall and unsure of themselves. A slight wind or a sneeze could bring them crumbling down on themselves and on any straggler unlucky enough to be inside. She goes through her options.

'Where are we going?' the boy asks suddenly.

She pretends she didn't hear him.

'Where are we going?' He is almost yelling.

'Keep your voice down.'

She turns to him, and he is puffing himself up, trying to make himself bigger than he really is. His tiny frame is almost lost under the large dirty coat he has on.

'You should take that coat off. The weather is hot.'

'I am fine.'

She raises her brow at the lick of sweat on his forehead. She faces forward and continues on the road, but when she doesn't hear his footsteps behind her, she turns back.

'Let's go!'

He folds his hand in defiance and twists his mouth. 'Let's go, *jare*,' she says again, putting more steel in her voice, but he remains rooted where he stands, unmoved.

In a fit of annoyance, she hurries towards him, raising her hand, and he cowers. Seeing his reaction melts her steel, and she decides to play along. Pointing to nowhere in particular, she assures him that they are almost 'there'. She promises him an extra can of sardines if he stops 'misbehaving'. The child mumbles his reluctance before he starts walking again. His steps are a little too fast, and she has to dig into her strides to catch up.

'Slow down, you this boy.'

Finally, they find a place away from the road, a large building hidden behind larger buildings. It might have been a church or a hall because there are chairs jumbled up in a corner and musical equipment covered in dust and grime. They come in through the only entrance not covered by fallen debris. The building is caving in on itself, but it would have to do for tonight. They reckon if it has stood all this while, it could manage one more night. They work together to move some of the chairs and pieces of wood to block the entrance through which they came in. Outside, darkness has fallen and with it comes a gnawing chill. That is how it is these days, the days are too hot, the nights are too cold, and the rains are few and far between. The woman rubs her palms together and warms them with her breath.

'Let us make a fire,' the boy offers, but she refuses.

'Someone might see it,' she says, thinking back to the gunshot she heard earlier. She sits, folding her legs underneath her body, and brings out a can of sardines from the polythene bag hidden underneath her jacket. The fish pieces smell funky and show early signs of rot. She gives it to the boy, opens another for herself, and then watches him as he eats noisily, slurping and smacking his lips. When he is done, he asks for another.

'No other one for you again o,' she says as she opens another can for him. He smiles a thank you and continues eating. When he is done, he lays on the ground, folding his arms into a makeshift pillow.

She sits back and eats him with her eyes, all his malnourished and clammy parts. His eyes—the way they bulge out of their sockets—

his nappy hair, his oversized coat that could have been white or cream under better conditions, his bare feet lined with blisters, and the little stub on his toe. She thinks to herself, 'For all his blemishes, he is innocent and spotless, pure and perfect as an earnest prayer, and whole enough to touch the Divine. Blessed are the pure in heart, for they shall see God.'

At night your dreams run wild,
Untamed animals dancing on the canvas that is the moon's plaything.
The moon an arc,
Is a night lamp,
Shaped like a hoof,
A paw?
Shaped like a shoe,
Shaped like something that watches over every other thing.
Shaped like a god's left eye.

The woman wakes to the boy tapping her softly. She wants to speak, but he puts a finger across her lips, 'Shush.' He points outside and motions towards the blocked entrance, his eyes alert and swimming with urgency. She sits up and strains her ears to hear footsteps outside the building.

Quickly but silently, woman and child walk over to where the chairs and musical equipment are and duck behind them. Their position gives them a good view of the blocked entrance. The footsteps grow louder, more prominent, intrusive, and with their hearts in their mouths, they watch as shadows hover about the entrance. The woman grabs a piece of wood and readies herself for the unexpected.

The voices come now, barely audible but laced with intent. They could be two, three at most. One of them tries to push through the blockade, but after a few shoves, he backs down.

'This thing too heavy,' he says

'Make I help you?'

'Nah. No worry.'

'If we move am now, this building fit just fall on top our head.'

'Abi,' one of them agrees.

The woman watches with apprehension as the men peep and peer into the poorly lit building. She watches as they toss and weigh their options before deciding that it probably isn't worth it and walk away, their footsteps fading into the night. All that is left is a still quietude, and the silence is an earful. She unclenches her jaw.

The woman and child remain awake the rest of the night till the early morning sunlight scours the building. Still, they stay out of sight, under the chairs and equipment. They know it is safer there; it is easier to get spotted with the sun out. It is safer to move at night under the cover of darkness, so they take turns sleeping and keeping watch. Sometime in the afternoon, a mouse comes around nibbling at the empty cans of sardines. The woman imagines the twitchy nose of the rodent as it expresses its disappointment. It must have picked up the smell of the sardines, maybe from miles off, and followed the lure of promise to this run-down building. She imagines the mouse's surprise at realising that sometimes disappointment smells an awful lot like promise.

As the sun begins to fall off its seat and night's black palm stretches over the dead land, the woman gives the boy the last can of sardines and watches him chew and swallow. Halfway he offers her a sliver of fish, but she declines. 'You should finish it. I am not that hungry.' With the honest ignorance of a child, he wolfs on and doesn't see the rheumy smile on the woman's face. She dusts the speck of sand on the side of his head and pinches his cheek. He smiles, licking the remnants of fish and oil on his fingers.

'We should move now,' she says when he is done and together under cover of darkness, they set out on the road again. Outside, the night breeze sings and blows much-needed fresh air into their lungs. The boy says it is better to travel at night, the air is cold but bearable, and there are fewer dangers on the road. The woman disagrees. She says night or day, it doesn't matter, there is always something worse on the road, never get too comfortable.

In the distance, wild dogs are munching on something.

'Maybe they are eating a dead animal,' the boy says.

'Maybe.'

One of the dogs raises its head and regards the boy and the woman, its inhuman eyes glinting in the dark.

'We should go around,' the woman says, tapping the boy's shoulder. 'We don't want them coming after us.'

And so they leave the road and head into the dead town, more burnt and broken buildings, empty caravans, dead cars, and people-less rooms. The woman is grateful for the emptiness because there is safety in empty. In their world, things that move tend to come after you. She reaches for the boy's hand, and he grabs on, and together they weave, sidestep, and heave through the crumbling maze.

You break,
Like dawn every morning,
Leaving pieces of yourself,
Trapped in yesternight,
Your uneven edges blaring,
And you hope,
That he does not see,
What you were before you had faith,
Before you had him.

Smoke trails at a distance, and the woman trudges towards it. The wind bellows and howls. The harmattan wind chaffs her lips and crusts her feet. They are sore from walking, taking more steps than there are roads to take. Even now, the road still stretches on before her, twisting and turning like an unending serpent. Her end might be near, she reckons, but she presses on.

Food and water are forlorn memories. Earlier, she had seen a cashew tree with bright red fruits. Her stomach had twisted and grumbled, but she knew it wasn't real. Trees don't grow anymore, and the ones that are left are brown and stunted, dead things still standing, just like her and every other person left.

The smoke is closer now. Just behind a building or whatever is left of it.

Then someone grabs her from behind and flings her to the ground. In a blink, her assailant is on top of her, hitting and punching and cursing. She coughs and spits and claws. Death is a cliff, and only those strong enough can brave its edge. At death's black door, a person who knows their time is up might still fight and claw, to live.

She heaves and continues clawing at her assailant. His hands are around her neck, and he is squeezing hard. She can feel her senses dulling. She claws and kicks and spits, and she hears him groan. She must have hit something important, she thinks. His eyes, his nose? His grip slacks, and lifting her head up, she sinks her teeth into the soft flesh underneath his jaw. Biting as hard as she can, she yanks and feels rubbery flesh and warm blood fill her mouth. The gush of red covers her eyes, her nostrils, and with a strength birthed from desperation, she pushes him off. She pulls herself up and, standing on unsure legs, looks down at her defeated enemy.

The man is clutching his neck and writhing like a dying animal. She turns to leave.

'Please, please, take him.' His voice is a deathly whisper.

She turns to face him but cannot bring herself to meet his gaze. She casts her eyes on his bare feet.

'Please take him to Byzantium.' He is gasping. 'Please take him to Byzantium. Please. Byzantium.' He struggles and coughs before his body stills, blood eating up the ground around him. He dies with Byzantium on his lips.

She leaves the dead man in the company of his silence and heads towards the thin wisp of smoke. Inside the room, there is a makeshift fireplace with wood that still gives off smoke from a fire that has been put out. She is vigilant, and her ears perk up like weapons. If there was one person, there could be another. The dead man also spoke of a *him*. There are empty cans on the ground and a heap of clothes in a corner. She picks up one of the cans. There is half-eaten baked beans in it. She scoops a handful into her mouth. Her stomach sings. In the periphery of her vision, she sees the heap of clothes stir, and suddenly alert, she picks up a brick.

'Who is there?'

Nothing.

'I said, who is there?'

Still nothing.

'Oya, come out before I break your head. One, two—'

The clothes give way, and a wiry-looking boy steps out. He is more rags than flesh, his eyes sticking out like they are too big for their sockets. He is young, too young.

'Byzantium,' the dead man had said. 'Take him to Byzantium.' The woman walks up to the boy, a stone in one hand and a can of beans in another. She watches him cower.

Coming down on one knee, she asks, 'What is your name?'

That place,
Where trees sing,
And the laughter of children blossoms,
And the Sun is God's holy fire
And the water isn't dead,
And nature is Eden,

And the name is paradise.
Byzantium.

Back on the road, the woman and child stand before a half-eaten corpse as the sun peeks shyly from behind dark clouds. The dogs are gone, but flies drone and hover over the carcass.

'It's a man,' the boy says. A question or a statement, the woman isn't sure—and scowls at the corpse. Most of the face is gone, and the torso ripped open by prying teeth, leaving the innards bare to other scavengers. The right leg is missing, badly torn off at the knee, and the woman sees what she thinks might be a gunshot wound close to the abdomen.

'Let's go. You shouldn't be looking at that,' she says.

'What happens when we die?' the boy asks.

What happens in the end? she thinks. At the end of all this—the travelling, the running, the hiding, the surviving—what next?

Back in those days, during the beginning of the end, when the trees and animals started dying, people lived with hope, a flimsy one. They thought things would get better, or more aptly, they thought things couldn't get worse. But they did, and soon the planet was dead, and it took everything with it. For the unlucky ones still alive, it was only a matter of time. So here and now, she tries to convince herself that after the end, there is just more emptiness, oblivion, a welcome nirvana of not existing anymore, with no memories. And no memories mean no more regrets. No regrets mean no more grief. That would be true respite.

'What happens when we die?'

'I don't know,' she answers briskly, stashing her thoughts and, taking the boy's hand, trudging forward on the main road.

As they press on, she notices that he slacks, turning regularly to look at the corpse even when it is too far behind to see clearly. She lets him be. She lets him wallow in his curiosity. The air is windy as if nudging them to keep going forward. The dark clouds get bigger, eating up the sky.

Up the street, there is a lot littered with cars, riddled with overgrown vegetation, waste, trash cans, and a giant billboard with an animated smiling horse pointing at the large building in the background. A supermarket probably already picked clean, but the woman decides it wouldn't hurt to take a look. She turns, and the boy is still some way behind, looking back in the corpse's direction. Sighing, she walks up to him and grabs his shoulder.

'What is the problem?'

'Nothing.' He lowers his eyes.

'Then stop looking back.' She pauses, takes a deep breath, and continues, 'Forward ever, backward never.'

The boy nods meekly, 'I won't look back again.'

She straightens, suddenly flushed and ashamed at her overreaction.

'Hey,' she touches his face, 'let's check that supermarket. We might get lucky and find sweets or Fanta. I know you will like Fanta.' She smiles at him, but he doesn't smile back, and she realises how much she wants him to smile. The fact that this child may have never tasted Fanta nibbles at her; she tucks the thought to the back of her mind, alongside other unsaid things.

Inside the supermarket, there are empty food racks, trolleys, and stalls. The few things left are non-essentials. The boy picks up a toy aeroplane and moves it through the air with his hand, making funny noises with his mouth. She smiles to herself because she knows planes shouldn't sound like that. She lets him play while she looks for supplies. After a while, all that she finds is some sour yoghurt and a can of corned beef. No Fanta.

When she comes back, the boy is holding a colourful kid's book, and she sees a stick drawing of a family: a father, a mother, and two children. He traces the picture with his finger, and she can see his temples tighten.

'Where is Father?'

She blinks as if gut-punched and wants to pretend she didn't hear him, but he drops the book and turns to face her.

'Where is Father?' he asks again.

She looks him over. He suddenly looks bigger, taller, older.

'He left to prepare a place for you,' she answers, 'for us.'

He creases his forehead in confusion. 'Where?'

'Byzantium. Trees grow there, and little children like you climb high up to pluck fruits.'

The boy just stares, looking, processing.

'Why didn't he just take me with him?'

'He had to make sure it was safe for you. For us.'

He blinks and, after some consideration, nods in what the woman hopes is understanding, or a semblance of understanding, acceptance.

'So I will see him when we get to the place?'

She walks up to him, kneeling to look him in the eyes.

'I promise.'

'Okay.' He turns and goes back to playing with the toy aeroplane, and the woman sits on the floor, watching him.

Outside, the air quickens and grows bolder; it holds something more now, the promise of rain. Thunder cackles, and the sky breaks open with light. The rains begin to fall, and everything—the trees, the dead land, the carcass, the dogs, the crumbling buildings, the woman and the child—heaves a sigh of relief. The woman and child hole up in one of the stalls in the supermarket, and as the storm beats around them in torrents, they cuddle, sharing in each other's warmth.

A GIRL IS BLOOD, SPIRIT, AND FIRE
Somto Ihezue

Scampering through the bushes, blades of elephant grass swaying high above her, Njika could see the Sanctuary etched into the mountainside—she only had to reach it. Across the shifting streams and the trees once men, she made it to the mountain's foot, sweat glistening down her neck. Njika had ascended Nyirigango's jagged terrain a dozen times, but nothing ever prepared her for the cold. It seeped into her bones, and the bison skin draped over her body could sparsely keep it out. Her breath forming plumes of white steam, she trudged towards the Sanctuary walls as hornets of crystal ice stung her face. Stealing in through a window, she latched it shut else the cold whirled in behind her and put out the torches lining the aisles. The sensation in her toes returned, and Njika ran. Past the great pillars ensnarled by blooming vines that crept up to the ceiling, down a flight of stairs, and into the archway of songs, its balconies overrun by hibiscus tendrils. Despite the cold outside, the Sanctuary of Nné Riliùgwū, *They Who Drowned Seas*, was as something alive, like September's rains had poured right in.

Getting to the Hall of Faith, Njika skidded to a stop. She stifled a sneeze. The daisies sprouting on the marble sculptures always did that to her. At the hall's centre, her spirit-sisters skirted a fire. She was late, again. An elder priestess waded around the girls—her hair, locs of smoke reaching for the stone floor.

'To receive is to—' Né Olude, the priestess, paused, as Njika inched towards the other girls. 'Where have you been?' she asked, her tone suggesting irritation but not surprise.

'Milking the goats, Né.' Squeezing between Dubem and Amina, Njika sat and crossed her legs in meditation. 'The stores ran dry this morning.'

Né Olude's gaze stayed on her, and Njika shifted where she sat. She straightened her hair, composed herself, tiny white flakes showering down her face. Mountain frost. To all the spirits, Njika prayed the elder woman's eyesight was as bad as they said. Initiates were forbidden from leaving the Sanctuary without a priestess. Orphaned like the other girls, if she got expelled, she'd have nowhere to go. She probably should have thought of that before traipsing down the mountain to go splash in the warm springs with the village children.

'To receive is to give.' Né Olude peeled her eyes off Njika, resuming her lecture.

'Né, what must we give?' Dubem asked, keen as ever.

'Everything, sweet child.'

The lessons ended, and the girls giggled off. When they crossed paths with an elder, they feigned piety, continuing their chatter with the priestess out of sight. All of fledging age, the age the spirits blessed the devoted, their excitement brimmed. Dubem had been chosen to lead the ritual. Of course she was. Dubem who the priestesses called Nwa Amamihe, her brilliance unmatched. Dubem who could sing all three hundred and sixty-eight palm hymns. Dubem whose robes were ever immaculate. Two years back, Njika had stuffed her pillow with cow dung, tricking the poor girl into believing the stench of death hovered around her. When the priestesses punished Njika, taking away her supper, Dubem had snuck her little slices of roasted yam. Nights later, in their sleep, Njika shaved off the eyebrows of all the girls who wouldn't stop taunting Dubem, calling her the priestesses' pet rat. Bonding over yam slices and shaved brows, the two girls became inseparable.

'What do you think the spirits would gift me?' Dubem asked as Njika and Amina plaited her hair in preparation for the ritual.

'The sight!' Amina gasped. Only a few had the sight.

'What if we are gifted already?' Knotting the end of a braid, Njika started another. 'Remember how I lit that hearth without any stones.'

'Shh!' Amina chided, peering around. 'That trick was possible because you read the forbidden pages of Ibídó Òkû.' Her voice ebbed to a whisper. 'You are begging to be expelled.'

'But—'

'We fledge when the spirits will it.' There was a finality in Amina's words.

'I want the sight.' Dubem smiled, and Njika twisted a braid tight enough for the smile to wither off her face.

The night of Dubem's fledging came, and while the Sanctuary slept, Njika yanked Amina out of bed.

'We could get in trouble,' Amina protested as they made for the Hall of Faith.

'I want to see it.'

'You will when your time comes.'

Njika ignored her.

They got to the hall. Its doors towering from ceiling to ground were bolted shut. Njika had no intention of using them. Adjacent stood the library door. Taking a pin from her hair, she poked at its keyhole, and when it did not budge, she muttered a spell, and the door creaked open. She threw a grin at an unimpressed Amina, and they went in, crouching from shelf to shelf till they reached the wall separating the library from the hall. From a shelf marked 'Restricted Reading', Njika reached for a book, the words Ibídó Òkû: The Curses of the Burned Ones italicized on its spine. Its covers were hot to the touch, so she wrapped it in her headscarf.

'What are you doing?' Amina couldn't comprehend how she was eagerly adding theft to the list of rules they'd already broken.

'I'll return it, later.'

Njika moved another book to uncover a hole in the wall. Peeping through, they found Dubem on a raffia mat, a red cloth thrown across her heaving chest. Né Olude, Né Achacham, Né Ekhosiyator, Né Binta, and some other strangely hooded priestess encircled the girl, covering her dark skin in powder. With tánjélè dye, they lined her eyelids. 'See child, see the spirits, see the waters that tether you.'

'It's starting,' Amina whispered.

The hooded priestess unveiled. Fifteen years Njika had lived in the Sanctuary, and she could count on one hand the times she'd seen the chief priestess. Clad in black raiment, a contrast to the grey worn by the other priestesses, her bald head shone in the light, the texts of the old religion spilled across her skin, her face lettered in a language unspoken. Nné Muruoha was a rare fey sight. 'Are you ready, child?' she asked.

Dubem nodded.

One at a limb, the priestesses held her. In their grip, Dubem was a hare caught in a snare. The chief priestess drew a knife, and Amina clutched Njika's arm. Over a fire, she heated the blade.

'There will be pain.' Spreading Dubem's legs, her hand smoothed its way down her thighs.

'Let the spirits guide you,' Né Binta said.

'Let Nné Riliùgwū hear your call,' Né Achacham said.

It happened in a heartbeat. A cut. A splutter of blood. Amina lurched, looking away. Njika did not. The cry that left Dubem, she had never heard a thing like it. It pierced the walls, arrows through clouds.

Staunching the wound with wrapped ice, the chief priestess threw the thin piece of bloody flesh into the fireplace. When it met the flames, something, someone, spoke from the embers, and the priestesses spoke back. 'A gift for the spirits,' they echoed.

Two moons passed, and Njika's eyes willed themselves open each night. The knife, Dubem, the blood, Nné Muruoha, the voice in the flames, they kept crashing into her mind like ocean tides. The circles beneath her eyes darkened with each nightmare. Njika wanted to feel something that wasn't fear. Amina had not spoken a word to her, and no one had seen Dubem, not since the ritual. Hidden away in the Sanctuary tower, Né Olude said she was coming into her abilities, and once she acclimated, a fledged priestess, she'd be sent out into the world to spread the teachings of Nné Riliùgwū.

Njika saw only one way ahead. As dusk fell, the sun straining to shine a little longer, she snuck out of the Sanctuary. Outside, she gazed up at its walls, at the spires of symmetrical towers gleaming in the sunset, at the empty windows like determined eyes watching over the valley. Nestled in the peaks, the Sanctuary, worn with age and snow, refused to hide. Step by step, grab by grab, Njika scaled up the walls, the biting wind fluttering her braids to the side. Blast marks and ash scars from old wars riddled the pillars, and the rough stones repeatedly grazed her knees. Still, she climbed. Mounting her body onto the ledge of a window, Njika stopped, breathless in the thin air. This wasn't her first time up the walls, but it was her first time this high. On the horizon, the setting sun poured out a sea of red, dousing the landscape in coloured fire, the clouds drifting right before her—maybe, just maybe, if she reached for them, they'd carry her into tomorrow.

Steadying herself on the ledge, 'Mepere'm!' she enchanted, and the window flung ajar. Inside was a room, the bricks of its walls a waning colour. And Dubem.

'Njika!' The startled girl rose from the edge of a small bed. Stray tufts of hair peeked from her braids, and the thin dress clinging to her body was many things but immaculate. 'How?' She limped up to the window, helping her in.

'Wait till you hear of the time I jumped off the Mosai falls.' Njika smiled.

Dubem smiled back, a faint thing disappearing before it could fully form. 'Né Olude spelled that window shut.'

'I've been doing some light forbidden reading.' Njika stood, hands akimbo, pride setting in her voice.

'Hm.' Failing at hiding a towel squeezed in her hand, Dubem sank back into the bed, and a hush fell over the room.

'The spirits,' Njika broke the quiet, 'what gifts did they bring?'

With her toenails, Dubem began scratching lines into the floor. 'Né Olude said I need more time.'

'Oh, I thought—'

'I knew you'd come that night.'

'What?'

'You're the only one who leaves tiny holes in walls.'

'I didn't know—'

'There was so much—so much blood. I should have prepared better.'

'How do you prepare for something like that?' Njika sat on the bed, her eyes going to the towel. The whiteness of its wool was dented with red spots. 'Does it still hurt?'

'Né Olude said I'd feel better in time.'

'How do you feel now?'

Dubem got lost in the room's colour, or perhaps it was the wall carvings that held her stare, Njika could not tell. In place of eyes,

Dubem had hollows. Like she was reaching into herself, in search of something, she shut her eyes. 'Njika, please hold me.'

'Oh, Nwanne'm.' Njika took Dubem's trembling body in hers, both their tears falling freely. And they stayed, in each other, in the fragments of their aching souls, and for a time, they were less afraid.

Night called, and the girls, still holding onto each other, said their goodbyes.

'I'll be back tomorrow.'

'I know.'

'And I'm sorry for the time I stuffed your pillow with shit.'

'I know.'

They laughed, letting go, and Dubem watched Njika climb out the window, down the Sanctuary walls, into the dark.

What woke Njika wasn't a nightmare. It was scuttling feet.

'What's happening?'

'They found a body,' Munachi, her bunkmate, said, leaping off her bed and joining the slew of barefooted girls flitting out the room. Njika went after her.

The last time an initiate died, she'd been attacked by a creature on her way down the mountain. A thumb was the only thing recovered of her. And though dreadfully unfortunate, the incident did nothing to deter Njika from her own little escapades.

Clustered on the stairs, the girls shoved each other as they stole glimpses of the priestesses conversing in hurried tones up and down the corridor below. The corridor soon went quiet, and one by one, the girls sauntered back to bed.

'Someone's coming,' Munachi announced, and they all came scurrying back. Four men came into view, a wooden carrier balanced on their shoulders. Men were barred from the Sanctuary and from their lives. It was a sacred rule.

'You must unburden yourself of mortal longings,' Né Ekhosiyator never failed to remind them. 'To fledge is to be above it all.'

But these circumstances were different. Njika recognized one of the men, the village blacksmith. On the carrier, the outline of a body could be seen beneath a white cloth. A hand slipped from under the fabric, and the girls gasped.

'They found her at the foot of the mountain.'

'I heard she was pushed.'

'No, she jumped,' Sade, the youngest of the girls, affirmed.

'But the tower windows are spelled shut.'

'The tower?' Njika rubbed the sleep lingering in her eyes.

'Yes, Dubem must have unsealed a window.'

The name surged from the tip of Njika's toes to the ends of her hair, and everything fell away. All the sound, all the colour, fading into nothing. Her lungs forbade air, her throat ran dry, and her heart clawed at her chest, over and over again. Run. She had to run. And she ran, and she fell, and tender arms caught her.

'Are you alright?' Amina's voice was an open present.

It flooded back in, the pale hand, the dim torches, the window, the one she unsealed. 'It—it was me.' A wracking sob overtook Njika as she covered her face with shaking hands. 'It was me.'

'What are you doing out of bed!' The words came first, and at the end of it, Né Olude.

Mice spotting a feral cat, the girls all scampered off.

'Not you,' the priestess said as Amina pulled Njika up. 'Come with me.'

The girls remained where they stood, and Né Olude, impatient and visibly agitated, strode towards them. Tearing Njika away, she dragged her down the stairs, the shaken girl struggling to find her balance. Njika had scoured every breadth of the Sanctuary, but at that moment, she couldn't tell where she was, or where they were headed. Through what felt like seas of aisles, she found herself in The Hall of Faith. The other priestesses, Né Achacham, Né Binta, and Né Ekhosiyator, gave way as she was led in, their glares eating through her. At the end of the hall, Nné Muruoha rested her hands on a raised slab. On the slab, Dubem.

'No, please.' Njika fled back.

'Quiet,' the chief priestess hushed her. 'The dead bare no teeth.'

Dubem was as a child asleep. She had been cleaned and pieced together, by Né Achacham no doubt. Once, Njika had watched the priestess stitch back a chopped-up rabbit, the threads she wove veiled to mortal eyes.

Dubem's skin still held the night sky, her face, a full almond. Unbraided, her hair was a crown of brown fleece.

'We know you spoke to her.'

Njika kept silent as stone.

'Gaze upon me, child.' The chief priestess lifted her chin with a finger. An eerie intimate sensation, Njika could feel her flipping through her mind. The sight. All her thoughts, memories, and dreams laid bare. Nné Muruoha let go of her. From a nearby pillar, she plucked a jasmine. 'You know why the sanctuary blooms.' She tucked the flower in Njika's hair. 'Our great mother, Nné Riliùgwū, clawed through this mountain, into the world. Where her hands broke, the rocks sprouted a garden, a sanctuary. The spirits of our sisters past live in these stones,' she said, her fingers tracing the murals on the wall. 'In every leaf and petal, in us. By their might, we are fueled.'

'And in exchange?' A pebble into a lake, Njika's voice rippled across the hall.

'You speak when spoken to!' Né Olude spun her around, her palm hard against the girl's cheek.

Nné Muruoha raised a hand, and the priestess withdrew. 'Power devours.' She took the jasmine from Njika's hair. 'Your little hexes and tricks may seem harmless, but without the spirits to guide you, they'll consume you, until all that's left is blinding darkness.' In her hand, the flower wilted away. 'This is why we fledge. In return for their providence, we offer the spirits fragments of ourselves steering us towards temptation, astray from the light. Do you understand?'

'A blinding darkness?' Njika's face could not decide between confusion and dread. 'What could be darker than this?'

Murmurings erupted from the priestesses.

'Once, we were many.' Nné Muruoha looked over to the four of them huddled in the corner, worry written on their faces. They too knew this story. 'Then one of us thought as you do now and sought power outside the spirits. It cost them their soul. Claimed by unspeakable forces, they wreaked havoc across the realms. Blamed for the actions of our sister, the priestesses of Nné Riliùgwū were hunted, murdered, and marked as demons.' The chief priestess tugged the neck of her robe. Carved into her chest, Ékwénsū. 'Those of us who survived now spread the teachings of Nné Riliùgwū, doing whatever it takes to redeem ourselves, to redeem the spirits.' Taking Njika by the shoulders, she brought her forehead to hers. 'There is strength in you. I see it. Help us guide your sisters, else they crumble and fall.'

Nné Muruoha returned to the slab, pulling the cloth back over Dubem's face. 'Now tell me Njika, are you willing to do whatever it takes?'

'Yes.'

Days bled by, and as Nné Muruoha bade, Njika readied herself. She spent her nights studying the scripts of Nné Riliùgwū, the utterances of the spirits, and to her sisters, she whispered words of assurance, among other things. Gone was the laughter, the chatter, and the sneaking down the mountain. And when Dubem's mourning rites were over, her time came.

Hair rolled into bulbs, into The Hall of Faith she went. The priestesses received her, laying her on a mat. Njika gazed at the ceiling, at the creeping branches and hieroglyphs, and she wondered if Dubem had seen the same things.

'Are you ready to give?' Nné Muruoha started.

'Yes.'

Like they did Dubem, the priestesses took her, one at a limb, and when their hands met her skin, they pulled away, screaming, their hands charred, the smell of roasted flesh taking to the air. Njika was as burning coal, like the sun lived in the lining of her body.

'What is this!' Né Olude shuddered.

'What I have, I give,' Njika said, and like a landmine, she detonated.

Thrown across the hall, the dazed priestesses watched as she soared through the debris and dust, the black of her eyes, the starting of fire. She stretched open her mouth, and giant serpents born of flames came slithering out. Né Achacham and Né Ekhosiyator were the first to perish. No bones were left, only ash and the echo of what was once their cries. Witnessing the slaughter of their sisters, Né Binta and Né Olude conjured a shield of pure energy between themselves and the blazing snakes. But with every passing minute, the shield weakened, the heat slowly cooking them alive.

Blood streaming down her face, Nné Muruoha stood in the chaos. And the serpents came for her. Bracing herself, she spread her arms wide, and before the creatures could consume her, she clapped. Like candles in a breeze, the serpents burned out. 'Insolent child!' She strained her hand towards Njika, and when she slammed her fist to the ground, Njika went with it, crashing to the floor. 'Do you think you stand a chance against us!' Behind her, Né Olude and Né Binta emerged, angry and scalded all over.

'No, not me.' Njika looked up at them. 'Us.'

Chanting into the hall, Sade, Munachi, Letisiju, Adaobi, Ugochinyere, Dumebi, Funmilayo, Daberechi, Nkiru, Amina. All her spirit-sisters. 'Anyi di Ofu, di puku iri — *We are one, we are ten thousand.*'

Thorned roots sprang from the earth, writhing around the priestesses as the girls chanted louder. And the more they struggled, the tighter the roots, the thorns digging into their skin.

'Né Ekhosiyator and Né Achacham?' Amina asked looking around. Her eyes followed Njika's to the pile of ash heaped in the corner. 'You weren't supposed to—'

'It is already done.'

Still battling the roots, Nné Muruoha shrieked a shrill piercing thing. 'You bind my hands, but my voice runs free. Across the realms, my sisters heed my call. They come.'

'We have to go.' Amina gathered the other girls. 'Now.'

'I can't,' Njika said, staring down at her arms. Branching across it, thick black veins throbbed like little heartbeats. 'They'd just find another set of orphans to mutilate.'

'No, we need to stick together. If the other priestesses find you, the things they'll do.'

'They can try.'

'I've lost one sister.' Amina wiped the tears fogging her eyes. 'I will not do it again.'

'You won't.' Njika's hand went to Amina's chest. 'I'll be here, next to Dubem.'

They squeezed into each other, and one by one, their sisters joined in till they were one big cocoon of little women.

'Go.' Njika heaved away from them.

And so the girls ran, out the hall, past the Sanctuary gates, into the mountain. Left behind, Njika crafted a ritual of her own.

'What abomination do you breed!' Nné Muruoha was not yet spent.

'Come and see.' Njika opened her mind, letting the priestess in.

'No, no—that is not possible. You do not possess such power!'

23

'We are the damned, the unbowed, the vengeful.' Njika laughed in a hundred soulless voices. 'We birth power.' Exhaling, a fire rekindled within her and engulfed the space she stood in. Her fingers morphed to talons, and with them, she slit her wrists, her blood hissing into the flames.

'Bia, ndi choro obara umuazi, ebe a ka unu ga anwu ozo. Come, you craving the blood of little girls, here, you die again.'

And they came, the voices, the ones that spoke when Dubem was cut. Like distant drumming on a hill, they whispered to her promises.

'No.' Njika drowned them out. 'It is your screams I want.'

With that, the fires roared, infernal, everything in their path coming undone.

Outside, nestled together, Amina and the other girls watched as yellow, blue flames swept across the roof, licking the walls and reducing the Sanctuary to rubble and singed wood.

'We should go,' Sade said, as waves of heat forced them back, harsh black smoke billowing up the mountain. 'No one could have survived that.'

'Just a little longer,' Amina pleaded.

'We need to cover more ground before the other priestesses come looking for—'

The Sanctuary gates blasted off their hinges, and the girls scrambled back. From the crackling carnage, a girl, hair rolled into bulbs, came forth. In her eyes, a thing, nameless, power uncharted, built.

RAIN DANCE
Lynsey Ebony Chutel

'Eina man!'

'Sorhrhry! It's not far now.'

The guttural sound of Benny's missing r, lost in an accent older than he is, is reassuring. It soothes the little slashes left by the dry, bitter grass as our legs cut a path across a parched field. There is nothing around but Benny, a short boy my mother says will not amount to much, but I know he knows this expanse of dead brown plants still rooted in stingy brown sand. Only the fat plants that came to this earth expecting nothing and carrying their own water are still green. You can see God put them here, on the edge of the Karoo, like Benny.

Benny is stout and sturdy like the stiffened shrubs we move over and around. He seems to glide over them, his scabby bare feet twisting around the thorns and away from the scornful shrubs. His shoulders weave in between bushes, dancing as he ducks the craving branches as we go deeper into the bush. They get their revenge on me, pulling my hair, scratching my arms, twigs cracking to warn the birds about me. One donnerse thorn tears my Sunday dress. My mother is going to kill me. We are beyond the barren orchards now and pass a flock of thirsty sheep trying to find shade. The schoolhouse, which becomes a church on Sundays, is far enough for the lyrics of the hymns to jumble into a dreary bleat of my mother and the other women.

'Benny, where are we going?'

He says nothing, only keeps walking until he realises I've stopped. He turns to find me, hands on my hips as my sisters and their friends do, except I have no curves where my palms can rest.

'I'm not stepping another paw forward until you tell me where we're going.'

Benny walks back to me, coming close enough to whisper, even though the sheep are now some distance away.

'You said you wanted to make it rain.'

I look up. A wisp of cloud too weak to do anything else but decorate the sky. The sky had been big and blue and empty for months. So when Mr Smit taught us the names of the clouds, he did so out of picture books. 'So that you'd learn the scientific names for the world out there, not the parochial nicknames your parents still use,' Mr Smit said as he made us repeat 'Cume-you-low-nimbus'. When Benny asked what purhrhokyil meant, Mr Smit hit his hand down with a ruler.

Benny is clever in school and would be cleverer if he didn't have to work in the afternoon lucerne harvest. He helps the grown-up workers roll up the spiky grass that will be food for animals who eat more times a day than we do. My mother says Benny is lucky the Farmer let him take his father's spot in the field when the useless donner just walked away. Soon, he will work full days. He is twelve like me, and it will be his last year in Mr Smit's class. Maybe that's why he tries to remember everything the teacher tells him, learn everything on the blackboard. He's even begun to learn some English words and spells them better than I can. I beat him in arithmetic, though.

'What good is arithmetic, says my second-eldest sister, Esther, when all Benny will need to work out is how little cents he'll make.' Ruth, the eldest, always laughs right before she says, 'Don't be ugly. Jesus is watching.' Sara, who comes after Esther and always supports her, usually answers, 'But it's true. Jesus can't punish you for the truth.' Maria, a cousin who has always lived with us, only laughs. 'Leave Jesus out of your gossip' is my mother's usual refrain before she warns me, 'Iris, I know you like your little friend, but you're getting too big to go running up and down in the veld with that little Griquatjie. And besides, he needs to go work.'

I am the youngest and darkest in a house of girls fair enough to get good husbands, or in Sara's case, with hair that could land her a job in the general store if we moved to town. When she thinks I'm not looking, my freckled mother looks at me with her eyebrows raised in surprise or her mouth curled in worry so that her face looks like a creased sheet.

My father claimed me as his favourite when he named me after his mother. My mother probably only agreed because I was as dark as her late mother-in-law. Still, she squeezed Martha in as a second name, 'So the Lord could recognise you as one of his children.'

'And when people ask you if you're one of them, a native, or an African as they say these days, you say no, you're a coloured,' she reminds me often. But who would ask, I want to say. The Farmer chased all the natives, or Africans, away when the Changes came.

'That's because our people are more trustworthy,' my mother said after the Ntshangases packed up. The round, red-earthed hut they lived in sits empty like a blind man with his mouth open, betrayed by the whitewashed two-room block houses we all lived in. Even in our village of five families, we rarely mixed. The fathers drank together, but the mothers barely spoke over the washing line and us children forgot each other once we left the schoolhouse.

'Is that why the Farmer dropped our wages to less than what he paid them?' my father asked.

Oom Siya was the last to leave, even though he was born on the farm and worked for the Farmer's father. I've heard Esther tell Ruth that she thinks Oom Siya went to a toor-doctor and put a curse on the farm. We're not allowed to talk about magic and witchcraft in the house, so Esther waited until they were both at the water pump, where the blue eyes of Jesus' photo couldn't see.

I wonder now if Jesus could see that Benny and I were not in Sunday school. I whisper a prayer of forgiveness in case he can. Following Benny, I can see his back is broader than it used to be, ready to hold down a sheep for shearing or hoist a bale of grass. If there will be any of that again. Mr Smit said the Karoo used to be an ocean millions of years ago. I've never seen the ocean, but Mr Smit once brought a book to class with pictures of a blue world with fish in colours I had never seen. He said this was here, in South Africa, just a few hours' drive. But South Africa is out there somewhere, where I hear the adults say things are changing, where people can do something called voting now, but my mother says the few rands my father gives her buy less than they used to. My father says he'll believe the changes when someone who looks like him owns a farm around here. I've been to the Farmer's house once, to fetch the Christmas box of peach preserves, sack of wine, and lamb knuckles, and he looked nothing like my father. The only thing whiter than him was the big house with its stoep all around, which was where Missus, his wife, made us wait.

Benny says he's seen white people in Uniondale, the town we'll have to move to if the rains don't come again this year. He says they drive cars and only walk in and out of the post office and the apteek, taking in letters and bringing out medicines. Their church is in the middle of town, painted whiter than the Farmer's house and even bigger, with a tower like an arm reaching up to touch God himself. It's probably why God hears them when they pray, I told

Benny. 'Maybe God is too big for our little schoolhouse church,' Benny volunteered.

Benny says there was a policeman too, but he was too scared to look at his face. His brother actually tried to go into the police station to ask if they had seen their father, but the police said they didn't have time for nonsense. Benny says the brown people, the ones like us, lived outside the town and mostly just sat around. If we move to Uniondale, my mother is afraid that my father will sit around and then start to drink the whole day, every day, the worst thing a man could ever do. For now, he only drinks when the sun goes down and on Fridays, Saturdays, and Sundays. She already says, 'Hy verafgod die drank,' accusing him of praying to the brown bottle like it's a little god when he should be in church on Sundays with the rest of us. He just laughs and says he doesn't need a church and definitely doesn't need that boring Brother Wensel to talk to God on his behalf. So every Sunday, my mother makes a show of rifling through my father's overall pockets and takes whatever coins she can find so that my sisters and I can drop them into the collection plate. It jingles like the school bell, warning us that there'll be a hiding if we're bad. My mother prays and prays for the rain to come. She prays for God to bless the Farmer with abundance so that he can bless my father with some work.

Each day the sky is big and blue and endless: the way I imagine God is when mother prays. He must want a clearer view of what's happening down here. Why else would he send the hot, dry wind to empty the sky? My mother, who prays three times a day and before every meal and cup of tea, says this land is so dry because God is punishing the heathens who lived here before and the ones who want to take over the whole country. My father says our ancestors took the rain secrets with them when they were chased away from here. My mother says not to bring that heathen rubbish into her godly house.

'Aren't we all the great-great-great-great grandchildren of those so-called heathens?' my father asked one Sunday evening. Then, he just started eating with his hands, scooping up the mashed green beans with his fingers and squeezing the rice grains into a stiff ball to mop up the marrow bone gravy, widening his mouth in my mother's wider-eyed direction as he pushed it all into his mouth. The light of the paraffin lamp reflected in the animal fat around his almost purple lips, giving his chewing smile a golden halo. I laughed out loud, rice still on my tongue. My sisters curled their lips like dried orange peel.

'I am no Bushman,' my mother said, shoving the fork back on his plate, before whispering with her eyes shut, 'Father, help us.'

The first time I opened my eyes during prayer, I was disappointed. I peeked through my right eye, then my left, then opened both eyes wide to see nothing but women, their heads bowed, their mouths murmuring, their eyes squeezed shut. Brother Wensel sweated as he shouted over us, patches damming into a stain around his shirt collar, his spit spraying like a summer storm.

There was no white man in a long white robe standing among us, his blue eyes open, his blonde hair flowing, his head to the side, listening to us his children, bringing answers to our desperate prayers. I wondered if my mother and the women of the prayer circle knew this, knew that there was no one there but us. Did Brother Wensel know? How could they when they never opened their eyes?

Maybe he wasn't there because he knew my eyes were open. Maybe that's why he didn't bring Benny's father back, or bring more books to the schoolhouse, or just enough rain to refill the reservoir. Maybe he knew he wasn't the only one I'd asked. My mother says he is a jealous God. But would he really be angry at me over a gogga, an insect so small I could crush it with my own little hands?

I found it on the windowsill one afternoon after school. It was just sitting there looking at me while I used Sara's mirror quickly before she came home. She thinks I don't know where she hides it when she's not combing and combing and combing her lucky hair, worshipping it. After checking my own bossiekop in her mirror, and probably confusing the spirit on the other side of it, I slipped it back into her suitcase. I had to lift each of our suitcases and move the stack of mattresses to get to it. The thought of Sara's face if she knew I used her mirror for my kroeskop gave me the energy to rearrange the corner we all lived in. I smiled as I covered it all with what my sisters called 'the wardrobe sheet', the frayed cloth we used to cover our belongings while we waited for my parents to lay-by a cupboard.

The praying mantis watched me, looked on as I tried to pat my hair down and saw me smile when I put the mirror back. I could feel it judging me. That's how I knew my father's stories must be true, that it was a god. So I caught the Hottentotsgod in a teacup and made a church for him out of my mother's preserve jars. I hid it under my parents' bed, on my father's side, where no one would see, including the blue eyes hanging on the wall.

'Please let the rains come,' I whispered when my sisters were out at the washing line or sweeping the yard. 'Please let the grass grow so the sheep can eat, so their wool can grow, so the Farmer can sell the wool so that we don't have to go. I don't want to sit around outside the town. Please let me stay in school, and Benny too, please let his father come back so he can stay in Mr Smit's class. Oh, and can we have new books, please. Please let Missus and her friends donate more books to us.'

The praying mantis cocked its big eyes and triangle head like Jesus in the photo above my parents' head. It folded its arms too, like the praying hands ornament in the lounge. It moved slowly as if it heard me and was deciding what to do. This god, my father said in one of his stories, is big and powerful enough to have shaped the whole earth. !Kaggen, he called him. And !Kaggen made himself into a small praying mantis so that he could talk to us humans, sometimes even play tricks.

After six days of slow dancing, !Kaggen seemed to be tricking me. The ground was drier than ever, and only muddy water left in the dam. The stream where Benny and I used to play was cracked and thirsty. The dust slapped us like naughty children, scratching our eyes and dirtying our clothes. It was a spiteful dust that seemed to know we couldn't spare the water to wash every day. Instead, the Hottentotsgod only moved slower. Maybe it didn't understand Afrikaans, maybe it was just a gogga, like my mother's blonde-blue-eyed Jesus portraits were only pictures.

Bedonnerd, I took the praying mantis outside where it belonged, setting it free to look at how the Karoo was swallowing up the farm, taking it back. Taking it away. Is this what !Kaggen wanted? Reclaiming his land? And what about me? Wasn't I one of his? No, my mother's voice reminded me, I am not. I am better. He was just a forgotten gogga, and the people who prayed to him were gone, chased away, defeated. So much for their god, he'd lost to my mother's god, to the Farmer's god. The praying mantis was already moving away from me, all six legs on the earth, free of his prison-church. I leaned over him, bringing a shadow over his little world, and crushed him with my closed fist. If I couldn't stay where I wanted to, neither would the gogga. I had to beat it a few times, its stomach splitting with a splintering crack like the pomegranates we used to throw against a wall, a mustard-coloured liquid oozing out. The insect's head was mangled into nothing, its eyes sticking to my hand. Sies man, stupid gogga. Its praying arms still moved around, begging to stay alive. Hadn't I begged it over and over? And look, not a cloud in the sky, not even Mr Smit's stupid thin cirrus clouds. It should have been harder to kill a god.

Four Sundays since my sacrifice and still no rain. Maybe Jesus saw me pray to the Hottentotsgod, so I asked for forgiveness every night. Didn't he see I vanquished the heathen god? Didn't my repentance count? No answer, except the dry heat that felt like the King of Babylon's furnace Brother Wensel preached about almost every other Sunday.

'Benny, I don't feel like going to the dry stream today.' We're far enough from the schoolhouse for me to begin feeling a hopeless thirst. I look back, and the schoolhouse church is out of sight, so are the squat rows of workers' houses. Only the farmhouse, with its curly gables, is still visible.

'We're not going to the drhry strhrheam, today,' he says, stopping to turn to me. His field bag is hooked to his shorts today. While our mothers prayed, Benny and I always wandered away from Sunday School, exploring the last little bit of bush that the Farmer had not levelled. We used to swim in the stream, but now we draw pictures in the sand. I don't know how many more Sunday afternoons we have left together. Benny seems to have grown even more. When my own chest grows, people, those people who always seem to have something to say, will start to talk. I have never heard these people talk, but my mother always seems to listen.

I follow Benny one more time, beaten by his enthusiasm and the heat. We cut across a fruit orchard and into a vineyard I've never seen. Benny holds the wire as I climb through the barbed fence. In time, we cut across a dirt road and walk across a fallow field until a thicket of thorn trees appears. There, in the stingy shade, is a mound of grass, too broad to be an anthill.

'Benny?'

'I heard about him from my brother. He's one of them, the ones that used to live here before.'

'Benny!' I say again, hissing this time.

'Irhris, you killed a Hottentotsgod. It's bad luck. And we already have so much bad luck. You have to make it right. Otherwise, it will never rain again.'

He was the only one I told. Not immediately, two days afterwards, when the heat was thick enough to sit next to us like a third person. He was more horrified than when I told him about the time I tore a page out of Mr Smit's ocean book. He said nothing though and went on drawing in the sand.

Benny is ahead of me, barrelling toward the hut, but now I resent following him, not knowing what he is up to. How would I explain if I got in trouble? That I let myself be led by that Benny-boy whose father couldn't work. My mother's voice, still singing hymns in the now distant schoolhouse, is loud in my head.

A man, who does not need to stoop, steps out of the hut, slow and sure as though he is expecting visitors in a place so barren. I have never seen his face before but recognise its creases.

'A heathen?'

'Shhh, don't let him hear you say that.'

He's already heard by the way he smiles. His brown is like Benny's but shaded in a way that would let him disappear into the veld around us if he wanted to. He's naked, except for what looks like a leather nappy and blazer too thick for this heat.

'It is Sunday today, isn't it?' he asks, catching me staring at what looks like one of the blazers Mr Smit would wear when he first arrived at our school.

'Mister, uncle, oom, we came—'

'*Tawades!*'

'Huh?'

'*Tawades!*' he shouts now.

'Uncle, mister, we, oompie, we don't understand.'

'Benny, this is a bad idea. Come, let's just go. If my mother—'

'You towns-children are all the same. Don't know how to greet,' he says at last, returning to a language we understand.

Village, I want to correct him, but Benny is again the better person.

'Sorhry, oom. Good afternoon. I'm Benny, and this—'

'Why is this one so—?' he interrupts, making an exaggerated scowl as he looks at me.

'Cause she wants it to rain, oompie.'

'Is she a Puchuchu tree?' The man hops as he laughs. A wrinkled face on a lithe body, it is impossible to tell how old he is. He looks like he's been around forever. I was running out of time.

'Do you know how to make it rain?'

He stopped now, looked at me, and smiled like he knew me. I stepped back.

'We all do.'

'That's it. It's getting dark.'

Now I am leading us, away from here, from this mad old-young boy-man who is going to do nothing but bring down my mother's anger like a dust devil. Dust. That's all there'll be because it won't rain, and God won't make it rain, and neither will this simple man. And now God, through a clear blue cloudless sky, has seen that I tried to speak to someone else's god, again. On his day too. I'll be punished, like the heathens. Benny, kicking up dirt, catches up with me. I hadn't realised I was running.

'Wait,' he pants. 'You wanted to make it rhrain. Well, people can make it rhrain. People like us.'

'He's not like us. He's a heathen.'

'I don't know what the church sisters and Mr Smit told you, but we are them. We come frhrhom them. My father was half or quarter or something, but he had a part of them. We all do.'

I look at Benny. He shares the madman's narrow eyes, high

cheekbones, and short hair that grows like scrub. Maybe he is one of them, but I am not. Not with my skin as dark as my mother's imbuya wood wedding kist, and my grandmother Iris's wide mouth and thick hair that defeats me each morning—Ouma Iris's revenge on my mother for taking her favourite son. We were all brown, but not the same brown.

Benny looks down. He must realise I am measuring his looks, his skin, his hair, his eyes. People do it all the time—in the fields, in the yard, measuring how to treat us by how brown we were. These things that seemed to matter so much to our parents, that decide who becomes a foreman in the shade and who wilts in the fields. Benny would end up in the fields, no matter how well he knew his schoolwork. They must have looked Benny and his brother up and down in town too. Maybe he doesn't want to sit around in Uniondale either.

We sit on rocks as the man rummages in his hut. We stay seated as he makes a fire in the blazing sun, still wearing his blazing blazer. Another one of Mr Smit's words: blazing. We sit as he passes around a handful of something brown and musty to eat. I say nothing when a bit of what I hope is grass catches under my tongue as I wash it down with what I mistook for water in a wrinkled animal-skin pouch. I hear my mother's warnings about potions and black magic, which always seemed funny because she rubbed herbs on us when we coughed or made cloudy teas when our stomachs hurt. I was always too scared to ask why they called it black magic. Right now, I am too scared to ask what I am swallowing. The old man seems to be enjoying it. Benny gulps it down.

'Now dance,' the old-young boy-man commands, pulling us up. He throws off the blazer and begins to sing and clap and stomp, his feet scraping a rhythm into the earth, kicking up a ring of dust around the fire. Benny follows, finding the rhythm quickly, his feet remembering. I walk behind them, imagining what verses from Revelations my mother would recite if she saw me now.

The dust begins to swirl into patterns, spiralling up around us into the sky. Not like the spiteful dust devils that slap us on our way to school. These swirls spiral up like arms reaching high, in oranges and yellows that glow like the fish in Mr Smit's books, shimmering in purple and blue ripples that circle around us. I think I finally believe Mr Smit that the Karoo was once an ocean.

Benny sways, dancing with the brown swirls. The old-young boy-man is spinning, a dust storm of his own. Their feet keep a rhythm that vibrates into the ground. The whole earth is a drum. The hut moves too, dancing around us. The sun bounds along. The trees join in, forming a ring like the girls at school make, hand in hand, branch in branch, skipping around each other, singing, humming. The old-young boy-man's mouth is closed, but I hear his song. It is nothing like the hymns in the schoolhouse, high pitched and bouncing off the walls. This song roams free, with nothing to hold it back, low like a whisper, sweeping along the ground in a vibration, rustling up through the trees and then leaping into the sky. The sky where my mother's God sits and watches me dance this heathen dance. I realise it is me spinning, not the world. When I stop, ashamed, I nearly fall over.

The old-young boy-man stops abruptly. Benny, still whirling, is startled when the old-young boy-man grabs him by the shoulders and pulls him out of his dance with the dust cloud.

'Did it work?' Benny asks, panting and coughing from the dust that suddenly tries to choke us both.

'No,' says the old-young boy-man.

'But we—' Benny starts, but the old-young boy-man is glowering at me. Then he bursts out into his hopping laugh again, immune to the spurned dust swirls.

'This one,' he laughs. 'She can't feel it. She's diluted. Mixed up. Mixed down. Mixed with everyone.'

He laughs as he steps back into his hut, cackling as he draws the buckskin over the entrance.

'Wait, oompie,' Benny shouts, trying to follow him. 'We need the rain.'

'You children are too lost. You can call all you want; the rain can't hear you anymore. She doesn't recognise you.'

'I killed a Hottentotsgod,' I hear myself screaming at the now-closed buckskin. 'I prayed and prayed, and it wouldn't rain. And now we have to move, and I don't want to sit around in Uniondale.'

I am hot from the endless drought, the confusing dance, the thing I drank and the tears on my cheeks.

The old-young boy-man emerges from behind the tan skin door. He looks sympathetic now.

'Look around you. Everything is dead. They killed everything. Maybe the gods saw you kill their messenger, but they've seen so much over the years. Meisie, the gods have turned away from all of us.'

Benny looks at me, and the dust on our clothes, and then up at the sky. It is big and blue and empty. I begin to walk away, and then feel my steps grow faster and faster, away from the powerless old mad man and away from silly Benny. I stomp across the fallow field, hear my dress rip as I climb through the barbed fence without waiting for Benny. I don't need him to show me the way. I know this place too. It is the only place I know. I cross the dirt road without looking and storm through the parched vineyard and the barren orchard until I come to the points where all the farms met, where our schoolhouse stands, now doubling as a church. Benny has caught up.

'Are you even listening to me?' He's been trying to say something all the way here, but I heard nothing. I look at his face. It now looks even more like old-young boy-man's. I hate him for it. I grab his pack and reach for the flint I know he always carries.

'What are you doing?'

I ignore Benny as I crouch. The flame hisses to life.

'Yahi! Are you going mad?' I ignore Benny and move to the next patch and then the next. Benny is putting out the fires behind me, but he is too slow for the dry brush and God's hot wind. The fires join flaming hands and form a ring and dance around each other, humming in a crackle.

The hymns in the schoolhouse church turn to shouts as the grownups run out. The men have left their bottles and are running toward us. Even the Farmer, who never sets foot near the schoolhouse, is in his bakkie, bouncing over scrub to get to us. By then, the fire has leapt to the neighbouring farms, pulling them into the dance. It is turning the white schoolhouse black, like a miracle. The women who aren't fetching water are on their knees in the grass, praying. It is too big for Benny, who finds me in the smoke, my church dress smeared with soot.

'What are you doing, Iris?'

'Making it rain.'

'What? Make sense, please! This is dangerhrhrous! You're gonna hurt yourself. All of us!'

'God might punish heathens, but he wouldn't let his own people burn, neh? Maybe now he'll send the rain.'

WALLS DON'T REMEMBER, HUMANS DO
Raheem Omeiza

I

You press your face into the warm glass window and take Lokoja in as the bus meanders through the sea of bodies—market women and customers mostly—spilling onto the road at Old Market.

The smell is what hits you first. It assaults you with an urgency that surprises you. You breathe in the air and smell the sickly-sweet odour of rotting fruits piled high by the roadside. You smell river water, the decaying waste underneath. You smell hot coal tar and sweat and the mustiness of a small, slow town that's not going anywhere. You smell nostalgia, too, thick and layered, each smell bringing you different memories. It smells like the time things used to be easy, of days spent running after old motorcycle tyres in nothing but underwear. You smell home, or what used to be home.

II

You arrive home and steel yourself against the performative welcomes you know you're about to receive. You wish they'd just treat you normally, your father especially. You bring out the chocolates and sweets you bought at the car park and give them to your half-brothers. They thank you with genuine smiles and quick, shy hugs before disappearing with their loot. You give your stepmother two ankara fabrics patterned in crisscrossing hues of green and blue, and your father an expensive handmade cap. A peace offering of some sort. They thank you profusely. Nothing has changed in your neighbourhood. Well, the lemon trees have grown bigger. The frangipanis have formed a thick fence of foliage around the house, and the green paint on the outer walls has cracked, most of it peeling off, leaving the wall half-naked, a faded memory of its former glory. Today is a Sunday, and Lokoja is content with its slowness and sweltering heat. It makes you restless, the heat, and you know this isn't the worst of it. The mountains framing the town are soaking up the heat and would give it all back at night. Your father indulges you and puts on the generator. He hasn't seen you in five years. The fans come to life, and their whirring drowns out some of the generator's noise. Your good-natured father asks you about school in Ilorin, and you fill him in, injecting an enthusiasm you don't feel into your voice. His face shows you what he is feeling: a mixture of pride and awe. He didn't go to college, so he treats college education as something novel, rarefied, unattainable.

III

Ali Close moves at a pace that's a little faster than Ganaja Village where you live. Okadas, keke napeps, taxis, and non-commercial cars are zooming back and forth on the highway. There are several shops in the storey buildings that overlook the Close. A boutique here, a showroom there, wares spilling onto small sheds in front of the shops. There are people, too, buying, selling, haggling, cussing, and pissing against walls. There is evidence of active life at Ali Close. The okada rider stops in front of your aunt's gigantic house, a colonial-style storey building. The rust-coloured walls bring back a lot of memories. You spent a huge chunk of your childhood in this place. You climb the stairs, run your hand over the smooth metal rails, and breathe in its heady metallic smell. You walk down the small passage, taking in the newly painted walls, and end up at the door of the flat your aunt lives in. You hesitate before you shoulder the thick mahogany door open.

'Assalam Alaikum,' you say as you enter inside. No one answers because there's no one in the expansive living room. The living room has been refurbished. This is not how you remember it. Its sleek cement floor has been replaced with modern tiles. The TV is a 65-inch Samsung LED flat-screen hanging precariously on the wall, not the big Sharp TV that used to sit on a short stool. You hear your aunt shouting at someone downstairs from the balcony, one of her grandsons maybe. You head towards the balcony to greet her.

'Mama, good afternoon,' you say with a smile on your face. You've missed her.

She turns around to look at you. She has to look up to see your face because she's only 5ft 4. Recognition brightens her face, and she hurls herself at you. You brace yourself for the embrace.

'Oh Hakeem, oh Hakeem,' she says repeatedly, too emotional to say anything else. She hugs you tight, and you hug her back, kissing her forehead intermittently. Finally, she pulls back, and you can see the tears gathering in her eyes. You reach out and wipe them off before they fall.

'None of that today,' you tell her with a quick shake of your head.

'You wicked child. I called you, begged you to come home, for me. What if I had died too? Ah, you wicked, wicked child.' She unties her wrapper, flays it out twice, and ties it back.

'You didn't die. You won't die anytime soon, and I'm here now,' you tell her, smiling again to soothe her. You know she's angry, but you also know she's going to forgive you for shutting her, everybody, out. And you already like that she's not patronising you. You take her hand and bend down to kiss her on the cheek, smiling all the while.

'Don't do that again, Hakeem. Please. Don't shut us out like that again.' She looks into your eyes as though searching for something in them, assurance maybe.

'I won't, Mama,' you reassure her.

'We loved her too, you know? Her death devastated us. We know how close you two were. You should have come home and let me take care of you, Hakeem.'

'I am home now. Take care of me.'

She pulls you by hand into the living room and lowers you on a couch. She doesn't realise that you're no longer a kid, or maybe she does and doesn't care. She goes into her room and emerges with a silk headscarf and a purse. She ties the scarf on her head with quick absent-minded motions, grabs her purse, and starts towards the door.

'I'm going to Old Market to buy some fresh maize,' she says. She knows you love maize and beans. 'I'll send one of the boys up with soft drinks now. Watch any channel you like on the TV. I am coming.' You let some time pass to make sure she's gone before you step out to tour the house. The new tenants in the other flats don't know you, and they gawk at you with questioning glances. The shed you used to play *war scatter* with your cousins has been torn down, and a generator house stood in its place. You try to pass underneath the stairs, but you no longer fit. You touch the walls, tracing lines with your fingers, willing them to remember you. But walls don't remember, humans do.

It is 2003, and you're a kid, playing *war scatter* with your cousins. You are all under the stairs, counting down from ten. Everyone disperses when the countdown gets to one to look for a place to hide, to take cover.

'Majid, make we no kill each other,' you tell your favourite cousin, the one that's only two weeks older than you. 'Make we fess kill Farouk and Sanusi, after dawan, we go kill Ibrahim and Zubair. If all of them don die, na we go win.' He nods. He understands that *war scatter* is serious business and that winning requires strategy.

The two of you hide behind a clump of banana trees near the fence and wait, holding your wooden guns upright with two hands, tense. Zubair comes out first, eager to make a kill. Majid sights him and is about to shoot him, but you hold his hand and whisper, 'Wait.'

'Pa, Pa, Pa,' Farouk says, firing into Zubair's chest. Zubair falls theatrically, clutching his chest. Sanusi takes out Ibrahim, who was hiding behind a metal drum. You and Majid come out and take out Sanusi and Farouk with a lot of pa, pa, pa. Sanusi sells it well. He shifts back every time a bullet hits him, flailing his hands in reaction. Eventually, he falls, legs bent in awkward angles, hands splayed wide. A well-performed death. You raise your stick gun to your head and shoot yourself, letting Majid win. He's happy, ecstatic.

'Hakeem, na we win. See as we finish Sanusi! Kai.' He pulls you up. Everyone dusts themselves and gets back up.

'Na me go win next time,' Sanusi says with a shrug. 'Na only Zubair never win.' Zubair is the youngest in the group, and he doesn't care about winning. He's happy that he can play war scatter with all of you. Zubair doesn't understand strategy.

IV

You sit on the floor of the living room, cross-legged, and eat your food. It's tastier than you remember. The maize smells fresh, and the beans is cooked to mush, the way you like it. A thin film of palm oil floats on top, swirling this way and that way in ungainly curls. Your aunt fills you in on what you've missed in five years.

'You remember Habeeba, the one whose mother sells *ogi* down the street? She's married now. Well, she got pregnant first, but she's married now. Mr Akin died last year. They said he was poisoned. They've demolished the old secretariat building and built a big three-storey building there. Mama Ephraim has moved into her house. You remember Mama Ephraim, right? She's the dark woman who used to live in that room near the generator house. I was so happy for her. God has been good to my tenants.'

'Are you enjoying the food? I made it just how you like it.'

'I love the food, Mama. It's even tastier than I remember. I've missed your cooking.' She smiles demurely, happy that you are happy.

'I make it with dry maize when maize is out of season. But this one was made with fresh maize. That's why it's so tasty.'

You finish eating and get up to take your plate to the kitchen. Mama springs up and snatches the ceramic plate away.

'Rest,' she says. 'I've made the bed in my room for you. When you wake up, I'll serve you another portion.' She shoos you into her room and closes the netted door. You sink your feet into the plush carpet and curl your toes. You like the softness of the carpet. The white sheets on the bed call out to you, and you answer. Soon you're asleep, dreaming.

V

You're four, somewhere in Ihima, clutching your mother's hand on your way to school. She's wearing a grey skirt suit and short black heels. You're struggling to keep up with her pace, so you break into a jog occasionally to keep up.

Now you're at home with your mother. You're wearing only your white underwear and sucking on an overly sweet orange-flavoured popsicle that colours your tongue orange. You climb onto one of the yellow chairs in the living room and look outside through the transparent glass louvres at mud houses yonder.

You're five, holding a brown, mid-sized teddy bear and listening to your mother tell you stories in Ebira. You are excited when she starts singing the song the tortoise sings to its mother to let down the rope from heaven. You sing along in your high-pitched voice, toothy smile and all.

You're seven, crying hysterically because you lost a debate contest to primary four pupils. Your mother carries you on her laps, rocks you, and makes cooing noises, kissing your forehead and wiping away your tears.

You're ten, graduating from primary school as the best pupil in your class. Your mother is there, ordering the photographer she hired for the event not to miss any moment. You pose with your prizes, happy, accomplished.

You're eleven, holding a pot containing moi-moi paste. You ask your mother where you should keep it, and she points to her head. You miss the sarcasm, take two brisk steps to where she's sitting on a low stool, and promptly drop the pot on her head. She's shocked but recovers quickly to catch the pot before it slides off her head. She grabs you by your arm, folds you over, and thumps you on the back for being rude.

You're fifteen, graduating from secondary school at the top of your class. Your mother is there again, her smile reassuring, supporting.

You're sixteen, in the kitchen, helping your mother pick beans. She tells you she's going to leave your father. That she's tired of holding herself back, tired of being unhappy. She says she's moving to Ilorin and will apply for a Master's Degree in Education at the University of Ilorin. You tell her you will follow her to Ilorin.

You're twenty, in your mother's living room in Ilorin, on holiday from college. You're padding across the living room barefooted, eating ice cream from a white ceramic bowl. Three policemen knock, and you let them in. You are puzzled at their long faces. They wring their hands, and one of them tells you there was an accident, that your mother is dead. The world falls from under your feet, and you're falling.

VI

You wake up just as you are about to hit the floor. A cold sweat breaks over your body. You sit up and look outside through the window. It is almost dusk. The sun has burnt itself out and is now a large, mellow orange globe on its way to hide behind the mountain. You go into the bathroom and rinse your mouth with mouthwash. Your aunt is watching TV in the living room with her grandchildren. They sit around her, fanned out in a semicircle. You don't want to ruin the ambience of this setting, so you stay behind the curtain and peep out. Well, until one of the kids notices and points at you.

'Hakeem, you're awake. You slept for four hours. Are you hungry?' She was already moving, on her way to serve you more food.

'No, Mama, I'm not hungry yet. I'll take some home when I'm leaving,' you tell her. She shrugs and continues towards the kitchen. 'Let me put it inside a cooler for you then.'

VII

It's almost dusk when you get home. The sun has extinguished itself, and a grey hue has spread over the sky, dimming it further. You go into your mother's old room from years ago and can still smell her in the curtains and musty air. This room is familiar. You know all the corners, the contours. You used to sit here, on a beige Ottoman, submerged under a heavy duvet with only your head peeking out, listening to her fairy tales with a face that shapeshifted to match her words. The small nail she hung her bag on is still hanging from the wall, unaffected by rust. You'd once hit your head on that nail during a particular unsupervised roughhousing session with your cousins. The blood frightened your mother so much she was crying as she held you while your father drove to the hospital.

The room has been left unused since she left. Your father never said so in so many words, but the separation hit him hard. He loved her—well, once upon a time, before their relationship fell into the quagmire of routine and cultural expectations. Their old pictures, long before you and your brothers were born, showed different people, happy people. He's not a man of many words, your father. Maybe he should have been. Once, she'd told you that your father chased her around the world to have her, to be with her. Relationships die. People die.

She is here, you think. She probably spooked whoever wanted to stay here. She never liked sharing her space with anyone, your mother. As if to register her presence, the window curtains billow lightly and raise dust that stings your nose. You sneeze, and then she comes out of the bathroom wearing her favourite purple nightgown, her damp hair bound tight with a white towel. You look around, wondering if you're hallucinating. She stands just in front of you as if she hadn't noticed you were there. Your heart is beating fast now, thumping against the walls of your chest in fear and confusion. But you don't run. Instead, you walk forward and reach out slowly.

'What are you doing here? You're dead,' you say, then reach out to touch her face. You touch flesh, cold against your fingers.

'Oh, don't be so dramatic. Of course, I'm dead, but I still live here sometimes. I'm buried just outside, you know?'

You shut your eyes and shake your head as if to clear it. When you open your eyes, she's still there, staring at you with eyes shining with mirth.

'This isn't real,' you whisper to yourself.

'There are more things that are real that you don't know about. I know you'll be fine, Hakeem. Now leave me, let me dress.'

VIII

You sit outside, breathing the fragrant lemony air from the lemon trees. Small streaks of sunlight leak through the trees and form overlapping leaf patterns on the floor. It has been two months, and no one treats you like an egg anymore. Your half-brothers are playing, chasing themselves around the lemon trees and laughing. They're happy. You work at their school now. You teach English Language and Literature there for good pay. You are not sure if you are happy yet, but you are in a good place. You're content and surrounded by love once again. It's not the type you are used to, but it is the type you can get used to if you let yourself. Sometimes you wander into your mom's old room that is still unoccupied, a souvenir of her existence, but she has kept to herself after that first encounter. You didn't tell anybody because they'll think you're mad and start treating you weirdly again. But she is here. You can feel her everywhere.

DADIMA'S KEY RING
Sabah Carrim

Although no one couched it in these terms, because no one thought of finding a parallel between two distinct events, Dadima was dying when Saadiah was born. Had one dared, another would most assuredly comment on the absurdity of the statement, since everybody, including a newborn, was dying with every passing second.

Dadima's first name, not coincidentally, was also Saadiah. 'Quite apt,' she said with a wry but weak smile. 'My granddaughter has come at the right time to take my place, to be *me* but in a younger body.'

'Tawbah, Maaaa, don't say that,' my aunt Nazneen shouted, causing Dadima's smile to recede, admonishing her for the bleak utterance and, possibly, for alluding to the Hindu belief of rebirth and reincarnation, sacrilegious when one is Muslim.

And yet, it wasn't that. Dadima was a pious Muslim and knew the tenets of her religion better than her two daughters and six sons; it just seemed the right response to disguise her shock that on hearing the news, she was not pleased but offended, not honoured but disappointed. There was nothing she could do except suppress the thought, feel guilty about being a bad Muslim (for feeling bad), and carry on as if nothing were the matter. Of course, we only learned about it later through Hussain Chacha.

My mother, one of the six daughters-in-law in the house, confided in me, making me promise that I would keep what I learned to myself and share whatever I heard and saw with her. Truth be told, I knew about most events in the house because I slept in the same bedroom as my parents, and they discussed everything before falling asleep. I even overheard and witnessed a thing or two that a thirteen-year-old shouldn't.

We lived in a big three-storey house—Dadima's two daughters and six sons, their spouses and children. There were nine ensuite bedrooms: one for each of her children and one for her and Dadapapa, who six years after moving in, died from respiratory failure caused by severe pneumonia. Before that, before I was born, my grandparents and their children lived in a two-bedroom house, slowly renovated to have three, four, then five bedrooms along with one, two, then three extra bathrooms. My mother recounted that Dadapapa resisted each renovation, a firm believer that the fewer the rooms and bathrooms, the more family members would mingle, confront differences, know, love, and cooperate with one another. He prohibited the locking of bedroom doors, saying it would impose a strain on relationships, and no one questioned it—not even spouses and grandchildren who came later. My mother said Dadapapa was a loving man but very firm and disciplined. He was strict about mealtimes, insisting that the family eat together. During the five prayer times, as often as practicable, male members of the family would congregate, female members behind them, led by Dadapapa or one of the eldest sons, Suhail Chacha or Ali Chacha. I was too young to remember any of it.

Weekends were spent cooking, playing board games, talking, and watching TV, the duties and responsibilities of male and female members set in stone. If someone had to go on a business trip or holiday, Dadapapa arranged for the whole family to tag along. My mother said that Dadapapa was reliant on Dadima to uphold these ordinances, which the latter did devotedly and told him gave her purpose in life. More than anything, he yearned for his family to grow and prosper, saying that Dadima gave him enough children to make up a volleyball team and hoping that they, in turn, would give him enough grandchildren for a football match.

When the time came, Dadapapa moved into the big three-storey house reluctantly, only because Khalid Chacha had to get married. Short of watching his favourite son leave the house with his wife, ruining the unity and togetherness he had nurtured and preserved, Dadapapa gave in to holding him and the rest of his children back. It was said that Dadapapa was so possessive of his children that, contrary to tradition, his two daughters, my aunts Nazneen and Noorina, were expected to live there after marriage. The latter conformed; the former couldn't find suitors willing to accept the condition. This created a silent rift between the sisters that neither one was sufficiently self-aware to acknowledge. My mother said that Dadapapa died very peacefully, confident that he had raised a family with solid values that would keep them united and pull them through any ordeal.

'Quite the perfect arrangement,' many visitors said, referring to the number of rooms in the three-storey house. 'So well planned,' a few added redundantly, not realising that the house was built *after* Dadapapa and Dadima had had their children, *after* Dadima was past childbearing age, so it was natural to suppose that their eight children would in turn marry and be allotted one bedroom each to fulfil their conjugal duties. But, it was *not* a perfect arrangement. Nine bedrooms meant no space for children born of unions, who grew up and eventually wanted a room of their own. Like me, the eldest of the grandchildren, the first to feel squirmy about sleeping on a rollaway across my parents' bed. It was *not* a perfect arrangement, I thought, when I found out how babies were made during a late-night interaction between my parents and realised that Parveen Aunty and Hussain Chacha had to share their room with their four children, aged one, two, three, and four. It was *not* a perfect arrangement, especially when Khalid Chacha's father-in-law came to visit from India and ended up sharing a bed with him and his daughter, Afreen, as hotels in the vicinity were fully booked. My mother said that he went to bed and lay next to Afreen Aunty who lay next to Khalid Chacha. In the middle of the night, when she woke up to use the restroom, a sleepy Khalid Chacha reached out and snuggled against his father-in-law, mistaking him for his wife.

No, it was certainly *not* a perfect arrangement. But people say a lot of things to please others, things they haven't thought deeply about.

For a long time, since she was much younger than me, Saadiah was merely another cousin, another addition to the family, and I refrained from showing unreserved delight in her presence. I was in that wannabe and, sadly, self-absorbed stage of wanting to be big, so I acted all grown-up to the best of my ability—sitting among aunties, asking whether Saadiah's birth was natural or required a C-section, how much she weighed, whether she drank breast milk, formula, or half-and-half, whether she woke up at night, and if so, how often. I was thirteen, and in many ways, dumb-and-numb, numb-and-dumb.

Saadiah was born in December, during our month-long school holiday. On weekdays, while the ladies of the house were out working in schools and offices, Noorina Aunty, on maternity leave, and Dadima were the only ones around, so it was us, the cousins, who had to entertain Saadiah. But like all newborns, she only drank, burped, and slept. It was out of the question to do what my younger cousins did: babble to her. Instead, I only cared to be around if an adult was, especially Noorina Aunty, who patiently (and impatiently) answered my questions about sterilising the feeding bottle, the water used for formula milk, the number of hours a baby slept, how that evolved as she grew older, and how often a diaper had to be changed.

Changing Saadiah's diapers, I must admit, was a nightmare. Her stools were greasy and foul-smelling, which made me decide then and there that having a child wasn't worth it. If Saadiah were not a firstborn and Noorina Aunty knew better, she would have deemed it a symptom of something serious. The six daughters-in-law in the house, including my mother, were also not on good terms with Noorina Aunty, believing her to be interfering, so they didn't have the opportunity to weigh in on the matter. Saadiah also had a poor appetite and a persistent cough that wouldn't clear up when treated, but it wasn't until her first birthday that her parents began to worry. At birth, Saadiah weighed 3.5 kg, and one year later, when the reading ought to have tripled, she was barely 6.2 kg.

Doctors were consulted. Some dismissed it, familiar with cases of over-concerned parents, claiming that average standards when it came to height and weight varied across developed, developing, and underdeveloped countries; that whatever Mauritian parents read and based their concerns on was unfortunately written by Westerners and consumers of McDonald's who were bigger, taller, and heavier. Others asked for a DNA test, then unavailable, urging Saadiah's parents to go to Réunion Island. 'Mauritius is the wealthiest country in Africa, and yet we have to fly to a small French protectorate to do basic tests,' said Aftaab Uncle, Saadiah's father.

'To be fair, not *basic*,' said Imtiaz Chacha, who was ignored and held a grudge against everyone for that.

'Let's *all* go too so that we can take Maaaa with us,' chimed in Nazneen Aunty, to which Imtiaaz Chacha remarked, 'Daddy's girl.'

Nazneen Aunty seemed annoyed by that but went on: 'The flight's just an hour long. Maaaa needs to get a proper blood test done, and it will be good for her to get out.' The other sons, Nazneen Aunty's brothers, concurred, except for Hussain Chacha.

'Did you ask Maaaa first?' he said. 'What if she doesn't want to go?'

'Who doesn't want a holiday? Come on, Hoooos, be more reasonable,' said Nazneen Aunty, reinvigorated by the watertight argument she just made.

'Change isn't always good, Naaaaz,' said her brother. 'Some people don't like breaks and holidays. Old people usually. They like to be in places familiar to them.'

Nazneen Aunty didn't like being opposed, especially by a brother younger than her. Noorina Aunty wasn't pleased either. How dare her sister suggest a holiday during a stressful time.

In one year, Dadima had aged even more, like a clock slowing down, unable to keep up with time, the process of decline pegged to the degree of curvature of her back and rounding shoulders. The doctor said her heart was getting weaker and recommended a daily course of medication but warned of side effects since Dadima was diabetic and suffered from high blood pressure. She chose not to take any, saying the sooner she died, the better, she would finally join her husband, Dadapapa, in Heaven.

'Tawbah, Maaaa, don't say that,' said Noorina Aunty, admonishing her for the nihilism, reminding her how important she was in the upholding of peace and harmony in the family, especially now that Dadapapa was no longer alive.

'Doesn't make a difference,' said Dadima. 'You're always on bad terms with each other and don't eat or pray together anymore. And no one's ever played volleyball, let alone football.'

'Yes, we don't eat together because we have different work and office hours, Maaaa,' said Nazneen Aunty, 'and we don't pray together because the men prefer praying in the new mosque next door, and you know women aren't allowed there. But *at least* we travel together, Maaaa.'

It was decided that Dadima wouldn't be taken to Réunion Island, although she nodded excitedly when asked. Noorina Aunty, Aftaab Uncle, and Saadiah made the journey on their own, and everyone commented on how things had changed since Dadapapa passed.

After Dadapapa's death, Dadima grew aloof, addle-brained, sour-tempered and even mistrustful, such that when she said or did something, everyone approached her through a lens of these givens. In one way or another, my mother said the family had written her off, that she had entered a phase where one was neither dead nor alive, since existence depended so much on validation and the social gaze. Dadima had also adopted a peculiar habit. In one of the deep pockets of the lengthy and loose-fitting dresses she wore every day, she guarded a key ring with twenty keys. They were identical in shape and size but had unique unintentional markings such as scratches, discolourings, rust, and grit. One or two were chipped in corners that couldn't possibly affect locking and unlocking—and if they did, maybe what they locked and unlocked was no longer important. Or if it was, maybe she was resigned to it. Dadima tucked the keys under her pillow when she went to bed, searched for them the first thing in the morning, slipped them into her pocket, and only then, opened her eyes, yawned, stretched, and let out other noises.

Dadima's whereabouts were marked by the jingle of the keys in her pocket. They knocked against each other when she moved, raised her arm to pick something, or shifted her legs to a more comfortable position. Amid the dreary and tense conversations about Saadiah's health and diagnosis, there were inanities about traffic, weather, what needed fixing in the house, playing volleyball and football (and how to go about making it happen), and not surprisingly, Dadima's keys, topics that everyone in the house could delve into, unlike the esoteric ones that Imtiaz Chacha brought up. Everyone wondered what the keys unlocked other than the wardrobes in her room and perhaps the cupboards and closets in other parts of the house. It didn't add up. We only knew what the keys were *not* for: the front door, the back door, and the gate. Because of the size of the keyholes. When asked about their use, Dadima said they were keys to the most precious possessions in the house and gave vague answers to further questions.

'Do you think we're sitting on a pot of gold?' wondered Khalid Chacha out loud one day.

'If you keep asking stupid questions,' Dadima snapped, 'I'll put something in your food, and you'll end up sitting on a different kind of pot.'

'Don't take it to heart, Liddoooo,' whispered Noorina Aunty. 'You know how Maaaa is.'

Dadima's two daughters and six sons discussed the new habit she had adopted, with friends and colleagues, complaining but in truth consulting, and were relieved to hear many claim that their old-and-growingly-senile mothers and grandmothers did the same thing.

'But why?' Imtiaz Chacha asked one day. He was the only one among Dadima's two daughters and six sons who didn't outgrow the habit of asking that question since he first did as a child. The only one who got on everyone's nerves. The only one who sounded wise and deep but wasn't street smart. And who got away with everything because he was Dadima's favourite.

Why do grandmothers get hold of keys and grow so possessive of them, he asked, and came up with several possibilities:

i. People grow weak and insecure in old age. They need to exert control over the little they have left.

ii. There is no reason. One shouldn't dig too deep because one may just get lost. Like in the search of whether God exists or doesn't.

iii. It's a learned habit. They've learned it from their own mothers and grandmothers and think they are also meant to do it.

iv. It's the senility. Makes them paranoid and do weird things.

Imtiaz Chacha presented these explanations to his brothers and sisters, asking for their views, adding that in his opinion, the third was the least probable and the first the most. I watched them insinuate in reply, 'You complicate everything,' at times literal, at times figurative.

Imtiaz Chacha caught Khalid Chacha rolling his eyes at the options and, instead of being offended, told him triumphantly that it was obvious that he, Khalid Chacha, was a supporter of the second explanation: that there was no reason for Dadima's new habit, and it was something to not dig too deep into. To this, Khalid Chacha rolled his eyes again, moved away, and decided on a few weeks' break from his younger brother. Imtiaz Chacha sensed it and in turn gave him an even longer break.

When someone called Saadiah, Dadima would jump and look in the direction of the voice. It would take a few seconds for her to realise that she wasn't the one being sought. Amused, we would watch her and, for a split second, notice the annoyance in her gestures or look before she would return to pretending nothing was the matter. We knew Dadima loved Saadiah—unquestionably—but just couldn't bring herself to call her by her name. Once, in a moment of no filter, I heard Dadima say that calling Saadiah was strange because she felt like a crazy old woman, growingly senile, repeating her own name to someone who returned silence or some meaningless gurgle or babble. When I reported this to my mother, she told me that Dadima had most likely never come across another person with her name.

Nazneen Aunty turned to Imtiaz Chacha that day, narrowed her eyes, and said: 'Tiazooo, now we know where you get that knack of complicating everything.'

'Shut up, Naaaaz,' he said, in an out-of-character response. 'You shouldn't speak like that in front of a child, in front of my niece. She will lose respect for me.'

'I'm not a child,' I cried. 'I'm fourteen.' No one seemed to acknowledge the truth of my statement.

Nazneen Aunty was shocked and hurt by her brother's harshness. Imtiaz Chacha insisted that it was wrong of her to speak to him in that manner. As a result, brother and sister stopped talking to each other for months.

Everything regarding our knowledge of how Saadiah's name made Dadima uncomfortable was kept away from Noorina Aunty and Aftaab Uncle, who had so much going on. But since we shared the same space, they eventually caught wind of it and grew resentful of Dadima and, surprisingly, of us—who they said knew about it all along but didn't stand up for them by chiding Dadima.

We didn't expect the outcome of the DNA tests from the laboratory in Saint-Denis. Saadiah had inherited defective genes, which accounted for her symptoms. A diagnosis of cystic fibrosis was made. No one had heard about the disorder, and in those days, there was barely anything on the Internet to look up. Noorina Aunty and Aftaab Uncle were in touch with friends in the UK and the US who knew people who had it, and were trying to figure out the fate of their daughter. The disorder, we learned, was more prevalent among Caucasians.

After consulting a specialist, we became more conscious of Saadiah's health. She was given enzyme tablets before every meal since her body couldn't produce any. Symptoms of the disorder were intense and erratic, such that she was often put on IV drips for weeks. Watching the fat syringe against her thin arms was heartbreaking. But this time, her parents were more confident since they knew what was happening and had medical terms to justify it. Unfortunately, the prognosis wasn't encouraging. Children with cystic fibrosis had a shortened life expectancy, and most didn't make it past adolescence. Saadiah's diapers, however foul-smelling, made no difference to me after that. I felt stupid for the distance I had kept from her and spent time learning about the disorder, how to keep an eye out for symptoms and tend to them. Noorina Aunty often burst into tears when we were alone, telling me that her baby daughter would never have a normal life like other children, never get the chance to have her own children, and maybe not even make it to that stage of life.

During that period, I also decided to move to Dadima's room, lugging my rollaway down the staircase to the ground floor. I had had enough. I needed my space. My parents were upset, but I was resolute. Dadima was anxious about Saadiah and, therefore, happy to have me around. While lying in bed, especially in the early hours of the morning, I would watch her go up to the wardrobe, pull out the keys from her pocket, struggle to find the right one because of the cataract in her eyes, insert it into the keyhole, turn and open it, rummage through the contents, and remove what she needed. One day it was a hot water bottle. On another, a whisk. Then, a woollen baby shawl. Baby socks. A blender. A ragdoll. They were for Saadiah. Sometimes there were things for me. Things that delighted me. There was no end to what she brought out of that wardrobe.

Dadima had by then overcome her discomfort in calling her granddaughter by her name, and asked for and about Saadiah more times than she summoned us. On many occasions, she drew out the keys from her pocket and let Baby Saadiah fiddle with them while babbling to her.

***

Saadiah passed away on a Monday morning, early in June. She was eighteen months old. Her lungs were chronically infected—a prolonged bout that led to multiple organ failures. The mucus membranes in her body were malfunctioning due to cystic fibrosis, and that had clogged her lungs. Noorina Aunty said that lying in a cot next to her bed, her baby daughter, weak, emaciated, in a final breath had said, 'Mummy, I want to go home now.'

I couldn't sleep for days after Saadiah was buried. I missed her and began to wonder about life and death, why we were here—why *I* was—why bad things happened to good people, and other matters that the people around me answered by making allusions to God and the hereafter, which sounded vague and familiar, rote learned and therefore meaningless.

On those nights, I would peer at Dadima across the room, watch her with her eyes closed, mouth wide opened, breathing heavily, and think about how vulnerable and unguarded one looked while asleep, how impossible it was to have any ill-feeling towards such a person. I loved my Dadima, no matter what people thought of her. My conclusion was that maybe the best way to get rid of negativity in the world was to require everyone to fall asleep and take turns waking up to observe people in that state. When I shared the thought with Nazneen Aunty, she didn't seem too enthused and said I had surely inherited Imtiaz Chacha's gene of going too deep into things and complicating them unnecessarily.

One night, as I tossed and turned in bed, I noticed the tip of one of the keys under Dadima's pillow, glistening in the darkness of the room. Dadima was snoring. I didn't hesitate. I reached for the keys and pulled them out. In my palm, I flipped them one by one, examining their markings, flirting with the idea of looking into the wardrobe but giving up on remembering how it creaked. I tiptoed out of the room to the kitchen, dining, and living room and attempted to fit the keys in the cupboards and closets—in vain.

When I returned to Dadima's room, to my dismay, she was awake and frantic and told me she had misplaced her keys. I was too fearful to confess my guilt. I went to the bed instead, took off the covers, and pretended to have found them. Dadima was relieved but still shaken. She climbed into bed, struggled to straighten the sheets, and insisted she could manage on her own when I tried to help. That was when she spoke about what I assumed were the keys: 'What they can lock and unlock is priceless, but the day someone starts using them, it will be the end of this house, the end of this family.' Then, she closed her eyes.

Dadima passed away two nights later. Of heart failure, the doctor said. I felt guilty. While preparing for funeral rites, the thought that the misplaced keys had perturbed her and possibly led to her heart weakening further and stopping hung heavily on my conscience. I couldn't bring myself to tell anyone about it. I felt a bit better when Nazneen Aunty came up with another explanation, claiming that Dadima's heart gave way out of guilt and sadness for Saadiah's loss. As we sat in the room around Dadima's body, now shrouded from head to toe in plain white cloth, Hussain Chacha confirmed what Nazneen Aunty had said. He was the last person to speak to Dadima, and she admitted to feeling guilty about opposing Saadiah's name, adding that it was probably why God had taken her away so soon.

Everyone lowered their eyes or looked away and spaced out. 'What did you tell Maaaa when she said that?' Khalid Chacha asked.

Hussain Chacha shrugged and said: 'The obvious, Liddoooo. How stupid she was to be superstitious. That what she felt had nothing to do with Saadiah's death. Out of the question to explain genetic disorders to her.'

The others in the room gasped and showed their disapprobation in other ways.

'Hoooo, how clumsy of you to tell Maaaa that on her deathbed,' said my father Shakoor, who decided not to speak to his brother again.

'Well, Shaaaak, if I knew it was the last conversation I'd ever have,' said Hussain Chacha, 'I would have said something different.' Nazneen Aunty and Noorina Aunty cursed their brother Khalid under their breaths.

'Did Maaaa say anything else?' Afreen Aunty asked.

'Let me think,' said Hussain Chacha, 'Not that I know of . . . wait. She talked about the keys. She told me to bury them with her or something. You know, the usual obsession she had with those keys.'

'Sounds like Maaaa knew she was going,' said Parveen Aunty.

'Listen up, everyone,' said my father, 'We need to stop this business of calling one another by these crazy pet names we were given as children. Shaaaak. Tiazoooo. Hoooo. Naaaaz. We sound like animals.'

'Say what you want,' said Imtiaz Chacha, oblivious to his brother's remark, to which he, my father, felt slighted. 'This had to happen. Maaaa was bound to leave us one day. We can't control death when it knocks on our door.' For once, everyone agreed. Imtiaz Chacha's siblings as well as their spouses acknowledged these words because they were wise and reasonable, and in truth, clichéd and appropriate.

I sat in a corner of the room, on the carpet where Dadima's body had been laid. Her stomach had ballooned up, and on top of it, right in the middle, someone had placed the set of keys. Noorina Aunty said it was to keep the gases in check; otherwise, the stomach could burst, part of the decomposition process. Imtiaz Chacha dismissed what she said as nonsense, to which she took offence, blaming him for his insensitivity at a time when she was also mourning her daughter. Imtiaz Chacha ignored her and explained that since the keys meant a lot to Dadima, it was done out of pure symbolism; there was nothing deeper that needed to be read into. This time the rest of the siblings cut him off, and Nazneen Aunty complained that he was back at *it*, offering lengthy and vacuous explanations unnecessarily. They also noted the dry and hurtful tone he had employed in dismissing Noorina Aunty, and told her separately that they were on her side.

'Maaaa's gone,' said Hussain Chacha, who held a grudge against everyone in the family for not being someone's favourite. 'Who'll protect him now?'

Dadima was buried that evening, and for forty days, the family congregated with the female members behind the male ones and, led by Suhail Chacha, prayed together for Dadima. The set of keys was put away in one of the drawers in her room and forgotten.

A year later, the family decided to sell the three-storey house so that Dadima's two daughters and six sons, whose differences were growingly irreconcilable, could go their separate ways with their families. Dadima's absence justified it.

Admittedly, I was thrilled. By then, I had Dadima's room entirely to myself, but I also had twin brothers who, not surprisingly, were conceived soon after I moved out of my parents' room. If only Dadapapa knew that this big house, perfectly planned and perfectly arranged, would one day be a hindrance to the growth of the family.

On the day of the handover, the new proprietors asked for the keys to the closets, cupboards, wardrobes and bedrooms. We found most of them, except the ones to the bedroom doors, and went around the house, searching for them frantically. It was around that time that I heard a phantom jingle and was reminded of Dadima's keys. I went to the drawer in my room, took them out, and went to the bedrooms, fitting them one by one in each of the keyholes of the nine doors.

This time I was right. Each key had a duplicate, and factoring in the one to the wardrobe, it made sense that Dadima's key ring held a total of twenty keys. I remembered what she had said so mysteriously that night when I had sneaked the keys out from under the pillow.

Yes, Dadima was right. Now that the new proprietors were taking over the house, they would surely put the keys of the bedrooms to use, locking and unlocking the doors. Indeed we would have moved out by then; it would be the end of us, the end of our big family of Dadapapa and Dadima's two daughters and six sons, their spouses and children.

GROTTO
Howard Meh-Buh Maximus

Babylon,

How is your shit life? Hope you are pleased with yourself now that you abandoned us in this shithole, flew to wherever the fuck you are, in the name of finding yourself. Ha ha, the fuck does that even mean, men! Anyway, fucker, down to more meaningful things. I just had sex!!!

And I know what you're thinking, but no, not with Eriqua. Witch told me I would make a good husband someday, but she doesn't see herself with me right now. You remember? How I was there in her DMs, persistent as a fucking migraine, singing Usher Raymond lyrics in front of the fucking ref, trying to convince her that just because I was a good boy did not mean I wouldn't be a good boyfriend. And then she went ahead and fucked Foss. Foss! After calling me Sweetheart here, Darling there, going around in circles like a fucking drunk's finger. And then she finally came around to tell me she was going to Mauritius for school just a few weeks ago man, and I know you would have been mad proud of me if you saw it, when I asked her why the fuck she would pass through Mauritius to go to hell.

Anyway, this girl I am talking about, her name is M'ayuk. Met her at this house party in Church Street just a few days after Eriqua flew. And we knew right then we were wasted as fuck because there we are, screaming to the deejay's shit music, both of us crashing a party that could have been thrown by any of the randos there, gulping some sour punch that could have been brewed by jamming up pipettes of all kinds of mammalian piss men. And then, just like that, babe leans into me, laughing and complaining like we have known each other since the Garden of Eden.

I swear I can taste feet in this drink, babe tells me.

Right? I say back. And this fucking music. It's like a compilation of all the songs you skip on a playlist.

You know how smooth your boy is, ha ha.

Anyway, we laugh, look at each other for the longest three seconds in history, and then as if it is the natural order of things, we drop our cups on the armchair and move to the corner to get away from the music. I want to tell her she is pretty men; it is right there on my teeth when I remember Bro Code Rule 14.3, *Everyone is pretty under party lights and drunken eyes*. So we just stand there watching everyone walk up the stairs, disappearing into the corridor. All of them in twos as if Noah's ark was anchored somewhere up there, waiting to save them, those staggering boys, those girls clutching bottles of vodka in their pits, smuggling them into new beginnings. That's when she smiles at me, really smiles with her forehead and everything, and before pulling me upstairs, she asks if I too am in need of some salvation.

I don't remember shit though, woke up on the bathroom floor to the smell of candles and not a fucking thing else. But this is the shit that happened a week later on my way to school. Met her again on the bus, and I couldn't fucking believe it. Karma is a waitress that serves seconds when you have no memory of the first. One minute we are smiling and eyeballing each other from across the aisle, eyes pressed on each other harder than the driver's feet on the pedal.

Next minute we are at the Mile 17 bus station, squeezed behind a cobbler's shack, peeling the clothes off each other. By now, the good boy in me had vanished like it had someplace to be yesterday. The rain hitting the ground is louder than a divine message. Men it was magic. Spiritual. Fucking out of this world. When we are done, we just stand there laughing, I am sweating in the cold men, and this leak on the shack's roof keeps channelling rainwater, dropping it on the sleeves of my uniform. And then she starts wiping it off with her elbow, trying to dry it with the sleeve of her sweater. If that isn't some girlfriend shit bro, please tell me what the fuck is!

Anyway, I look at her now and think she is certainly pretty, her cheeks puff, chin narrow, and eyes this big. She looks at my uniform and asks me if I go to Saint Joseph. I want to say no, but the only thing lamer than agreeing to babe that you're a high school student is letting babe think you woke up one rainy morning and decided to throw on someone else's high school uniform. So I say yes, with this grin that I promise doesn't make me look foolish, I have practised it, it is kind of cute if I may say so myself. So then, babe tells me she has a brother in Saint Joseph as well. Says his name is Carl Etchi or Cal Etchi or something and that he is just starting this year. Can I please, please, please look out for him? I fucking told you men, girlfriend shit! But then she asks me not to mention this, or her, to her brother, only because the kid can be a little weird about these things.

Of course, of course, I say, but I am also thinking her brother is not weird at all; I too would kill any bastard senior who was messing around with my sister in open spaces.

So when we are about to space, I ask for babe's number, and she asks why I have a phone in school. I tell her I'm in Lower Sixths bitch, and she laughs, asks if Lower Sixth students are allowed phones in Saint Joseph.

No ma, I tell her laughing, but they are sharp enough to know how to smuggle in all the things they want.

And I can see it in her eyes man, girls eat up that shit, Eriqua, M'ayuk, I can see that she is thrilled by this, the street cred of a rebellious teenager. And before we part, babe hugs me and everything, palms on my back for what feels like days, holds me tighter than a fucking grudge. She tells me she is expecting my call, and I tell her of course, of course. Even though, you know me men, can swear I didn't have even the casing of a phone, ha ha, only a SIM card that I had slipped in my wallet, hoping to rent a phone from those students who had balls big enough to smuggle in contrabands bigger than SIM cards.

And so in the dorm last night, while those retards flocked around with their noisy welcomes, their Yo Mens and How Was Your Hols rants, I retired into my bed men, waved away the students who had decided that telling their vacation stories was a matter of life and death, blocked the whole fucking porch with lockers and suitcases, and then sat up to draw M'ayuk before this rowdy shithole made me forget what the hell she looked like.

Yo Babylon,

I got the money you sent me. Thanks man. You're loyal. See, this is why I love this whole vow of poverty thing you all are taking. Friends like me who are 'the poor' get to keep all of your money. Ha ha. Listen, I am not even judging, but you know only those who have never seen real poverty will so readily commit to it yeah? It is ugly fam. But then again, what do I know about ugly? Isn't it in the eye of the beholder or some bullshit?

But really men, how is it over there? The rain here has been mighty pompous since June, showing up every fucking day like some stalker. And the runoffs men, those are only second to the amount of tears you cried when what's-her-face dumped your ass last year. Ha ha. Don't go on a rampage bitch, it's a joke. And aren't you some kind of seminarian now, or a monk, or something? You can't be mad at these things anymore. Higher power and all. Ha ha.

Anyway, back to me. You know I really did need to meet this Cal Etchi kid yeah, so I invited the entire batch of Form One students to my dormitory. You remember how they used to do us back then? Have us kneel and ask if we had pretty elder sisters? Of course you remember, why wouldn't you? You always got away men, culling up favours from those fuckers because of Jamila, while the rest of us knelt on the cold concrete floor, hands in the air, cursing our parents for giving us only brothers we couldn´t pimp out for school favours.

And so I scan through the juniors, passively waiting to get to this Cal kid. I needed to get information on M'ayuk without making it obvious that I knew her. You know how we do. But then I reach this kid, ask if he has a pretty elder sister, and boy just kneels there, staring at me dead in the eye like a fucking owl. Unblinking. His sister was right fam, the kid is weird as shit.

The next day I summon him, send him to go fetch me water to drink. The kid lodges in Saint Kitts, three blocks away from me. He sleeps on the bunk above Rulez and never answers when you talk to him, just stands there staring like he is mute or something. The tap is three minutes from me but like six from him. Don't ask me why I know this. You of all people know how this school can bore one to insanity. I watch him though. There is a queue, but all it takes is for one person to cut through it and then it becomes survival of the fittest. But he doesn't fight, doesn't tussle with the rest of them, he just stands there watching the battle of who will fetch before whom, holding my bottle flimsily in a corner as if my thirst was a virtue he was not in a hurry to tamper with. When he returns, I take the bottle from him and empty it on the lawn before asking him to go get ready for preps. He looks at the water he'd spent twenty minutes of his siesta time fetching, it is glistering on the grass like dew, he looks up at me, and then wordlessly, he turns around and leaves.

That night, I hide by the slabs behind the dorm where we bathe when we bathe outside, and call M'ayuk for the first time. The security lights are still broken, and the only thing shining is the Motorola I got from Rulez. I talk in my deepest, most unnatural voice as if she has never heard me talk before. We go on and on, humming sugary nothings into each other's ears. When she asks about her brother, I want to tell her that I had caught him spitting in the water I asked him to fetch me. How when he handed me the bottle, and I saw the thick layer of bubbles floating on the water, it was the thought of her, M'ayuk, that had stopped me from beating the spittle in his body dry. But I don't tell her this, instead I say, Cal? He is a little too much, that one.

And then I laugh as if it was meant to be a joke. But for the first time, M'ayuk doesn't laugh with me. She tells me her brother has been through a bit for a thirteen-year-old. Could I please be patient with him, help him?

What happened? I ask, but then she just sighs this heavy sigh like someone trying to get rid of some weight that just won't go.

It is not something I can talk about now, she tells me, and it is in the way she says it bro, the serious calm of her voice, so different from the person I have known her to be, it is the quiet plea that makes me promise to try, to really try, to take care of Cal.

In the days after, this kid and I create this fucking cycle, man. Every day, I call him and send him to fetch me water to drink, and every day, it comes back with bubbles of spittle. I empty the bottle on the lawn and quietly ask him to get ready for preps.

Hey Babylonian,

Motherfucker, I saw your last letter about Eriqua. Ha ha, I see you've got jokes now. Well, as you know very well, I am over that traitor. So over her I am cool with Foss now. Even had the motherfucker talk to M'ayuk once, just to tell you how over Eriqua I am. But then, before I knew it, your guy Foss had taken the phone to a corner and started talking all soft and shit, beating around the bush, dragging his words the way you do when you are trying to make a short story long.

Allô ma chérie, in this French accent so fake, if you dipped it in water, it would turn the entire bucket red. Dude even went ahead to tell her she was magnifique, someone he had never even seen before. I tell you most solemnly Emilio, the only thing more pathetic than that charlatan is your Makossa dance moves.

But talking about M'ayuk, men!!! Things have been developing faster than those drama series on Novella, plot thickening like pap left in the cold. Don't ask me how, but babe has created this system where she comes to school to see me through the ram. Every weekend, we fuck in the potato farm until I literally want to die. And then we smoke the weed she comes with and just lie there on the beds meant for yams. And then some bell goes and reminds us that she too has to.

As for her brother, I am still trying to pinpoint what the fuck is wrong with him. You know he goes to the grotto every other day with a candle? Yes, the same grotto we built last year as punishment, all those stones we carried on our backs to build a shrine that nobody goes to. Well, except Cal Etchi. The first time I saw him there, I almost dropped. I had just finished with his sister, and there he was, kneeling, dropping candle wax on the stones, reciting what sounded like a poem, a prayer. I won't lie to you men, it scared the shit out of me just because what the fuck! When I asked him what he was doing there all by himself, it is the first time he speaks to me. Tells me some deep shit about how when one has so many questions and sees no one to answer them, they turn to someone they cannot see. And I know that shit would probably sound fucking banal if any of us said it, but it was his eyes men, the words chopping out of his small body like something heavy, something shredded.

Yo Babylon,

Handover just passed a week ago, and it is funny because Rulez and I spent a lot of that period talking about you. I personally think with the way you were beaten in this school, you had every right to leave, go find yourself somewhere far because, yes it is true, these guys almost finished you here. Ha ha.

Do you remember how you got slapped on our first handover here? How it left fingerprints on your cheek? How no matter how terrified we were of those seniors, we couldn't stop laughing because Foss kept making all those white jokes, and you kept saying you weren't white, that you were biracial, mother brown, father black, as if anybody fucking cared. Ha ha. It was the one time he was close to funny, and you know your stupefied reactions were what helped him. Now I regret laughing at his jokes that day because five years later and the fucker still thinks he is Basket Mouth.

Do you know he was vying for Sanitation Prefect? But because he thought I was going for Socials, he decided to go for that too. When after we submitted our applications, I told him I just want to be Clubs Prefect so I could help the art scene around here, fucker's already dropped face re-dropped like a fucking pan. I have never seen a person so determined to only want the things I want. It is spiritual, I tell you. So maybe we need a ritual. Maybe we need to wash him in my piss or something. Perhaps it would curb this desperate cock-blocking.

And you know these kids think he is cool? That Cal Etchi and I sort of got close around this handover time. And during the campaign, I asked him what he thought of Foss as a prefect. It was still the bonbon phase, when we share sweets and biscuits to cajole them to vote for us, and truly, I was slightly disappointed when kid told me Foss was really cool, gave them Mambo and everything. Does that remind you of anything? Of anyone? Fucking Senior What's-his-name. The one who was Angel Gabriel, pre-handover, only to turn around later and ask us to address him as Emperor Yes Emperor. Both because only one Emperor was one Emperor too few, and what disrespect for a boy of all his five foot two caliber! Foss is a déjà vu of that fucker. A shit sandwich. A curse in disguise.

They found out pretty soon after the handover. Foss gathered them in the box room, and when I got there, I asked Cal to go kneel on my porch. He thought he was dead, that I would crucify him for all the spitting in my water. And you know I would have, if not for M'ayuk. Anyway, that is how we got talking. He showed me some of his poems, and you can call me bitch all you want, but poetry is beautiful. Otherworldly. I asked him if he was interested in sharing it with the school during socials. He thought about it for a while and said maybe. And then the kid smiled. He fucking smiled. His eyes lighting up like M'ayuk's, and I could not believe it.

M'ayuk and I have become five and six, and I smell her even in her absence. Babe smells like candle wax. It makes zero sense. We meet at the potato farm still, and sometimes I draw her before we fuck, soil painting the portrait of her face beneath us. She thanks me for her brother, who now slides me poems to read and fetches my water before I ask. He has a spare key to my locker and, every so often, rummages it for milk and Parle-G. We small talk in the corridors of his classroom during breaks, and he finishes my plate of rice on Tuesdays and Thursdays. Sometimes, he falls asleep on my bed, and I stay up drawing because this new quiet is that of a stream finding its way into an ocean. I know, I know, I have been reading too much poetry, but you can't fucking tell me I am romanticising shit. It would be rich coming from someone who has canonised poverty. Ha ha.

Hi Emilio

I know I haven't written to you in a while, but it has been crazy out here. Something happened, and I cannot even open my mouth to say it. Nobody knows. Not even Rulez. And I am writing this because I need to tell someone, someone close, someone far, someone who couldn't look at me the way I know anyone would if I told them face-à-face. So yeah, apparently, M'ayuk is dead. Has been dead for a while now. Dead before the last letter I sent you. Before the bus ride and the sex by the shack. Babe had been dead before we fucking met at the party in Church Street. I know what you're thinking. But no, it is not a joke. I have been thinking about this for weeks since Cal Etchi told me. Since he showed me. I have been trying to understand.

He'd found drawings of her in my locker while milk-hunting. I had just left M'ayuk on the farm that Saturday evening and rushed to the dorm to find him sitting on my bed, clutching the drawings like documents of something valuable we'd both lost. He was quiet. Asked, so I knew his sister, and I had heard myself stammer. It is funny now that I think about it; he is so small, so powerless before me, and yet it was I who was stammering.

And then he got up and started pacing around my compartment, biting his fingers. We were quiet for a while; I thought he was angry at me, that I was fucking his sister and keeping it from him. But then he turned around and faced me, and I saw the tears. I was still juggling frozen thoughts when he walked up to me and hugged me, burying his face in my chest. And I just stood there like what the fuck is happening now!

The next few hours were the most confusing of my life. First, he told me about the loss of his entire family. His mother, father, and sister had been shot dead by unknown gunmen. And then he ran to Saint Kitts, returned with this album of M'ayuk's funeral, dated about three years ago. Well, M'ayuk and his parents. And I froze, man, at the picture of the girl in the coffin, the same girl I had just been with hours ago, who had kissed me on the nose, laughed in my face and pulled out the weed. Whom I had drawn, head thrown back, boobs out, as she blew the smoke upwards, making rings. I still had the fucking drawing in my hand.

I didn't know you two were close, the kid said finally, cleaning his eyes, cutting into my confusion, releasing his last sniffle and trying to replace it with this sad chuckle. I used to wonder why you were always so protective of me.

Weeks have passed, and we are on break now. I still have not stopped thinking about it. Have not stopped wondering what it meant, that the only person I have been with, only person I had caught myself loving, was not even real. Or was she?

I haven't been going out much. Haven't been able to. But Cal Etchi came to visit me yesterday. To tell me about this poetry event he'll be performing at, could I please come?

Yes! I say and fistbump him, tell him I am proud of him, I'll definitely be there.

It was interesting to see him out of his uniform. He wore jean shorts and an orange shirt, and this haircut that meant one of two things: his barber either fucking disliked him or just had a dark sense of humour. So I took him to Killian Kutz to correct his hairline and fix his face. And when he looked in the mirror later, he nodded to himself as if the haircut change had all been his idea.

When we're done, I took him to Mitochondrion, this new snack bar by the ocean that sells food during the day and transforms into a club at night. We sat there eating suya, drinking Malta. The quiet, the breeze, the soft music in the back like a soundtrack of our lives. It was an ambience for deep talk, and many boys brought girls out here to convince them of their affection, of what they had been meaning to tell them. It occurred to me then, watching the couples smiling awkwardly, or clinging to each other, that M'Ayuk and I had never really been out on a date like this, to a place like this. And so I asked him, the one question that had been on my mind ever since I learned of M'Ayuk's death. Asked him if he believed that people returned from the dead for any reason whatsoever—love, care, revenge?

And it had startled me, the franticness of his no, no bloody way! That's all movie stuff, and not the good kind.

And I had said quietly that I knew someone. That was when he looked at me, and I had tried then to act as non-pensive, as flippant about the statement as much as I could. Like it wasn't anything deep, anything out of this world. Like dead people returned to us as often as Tuesdays did. And then for the first time in my life, I heard Cal Etchi laugh, like really laugh. I had seen him smile, heard him chuckle, maybe even a soft too-long giggle, but this was different. He laughed now with his head thrown back like M'ayuk used to, his chest heaving, hitting our table, almost choking on his drink. He laughed and laughed, only pausing for air, pausing to say 'grand frère, no disrespect at all, no disrespect ever, but you have to lay off that grass you've been smoking, you know I found some in your locker.'

And when he went back to laughing, his eyes watering, I thought of how ridiculous I must have sounded, how ridiculous I must have seemed, so I joined him and laughed too, my laugh building slowly to catch up with his, as if everything I had experienced, everything I had said, everything at all, had been a joke.

THE WAY OF GODS
Mazpa Ejikem

This is a story of a mother and her daughter and her daughter's daughter.

This is a story about us; we are many, and we are one.

This is a story spanning generations, and it begins and ends in the Old Forest.

Old Forest

pronunciation [IPA]: /ˈəʊld ˈfɒɹɪst/

noun (uncountable)

the wondrous magnificence of dense trees in Awo Community, wedged between Ekwe and Umuosu Villages. It takes its origin from a body of freshwater—the Njaba river—and tumbles into the clouds.

Example: Long, long ago, even before salt-skinned men stomped hands and feet into our world, before they belittled our story with their silvery tongues and bulldozed our past with their glossy refinement, there was the **Old Forest.**

Synonyms: Oke-Ofia, Evil Forest.

Some afternoons, the sun drifts to the centre of the clear sky and bakes the earth in its sweltering heat. Little children do not go out to play. The dogs lie on their bellies and soak in the warmth outside.

Birds find rest on tall trees and rooftops, and everything throws bloated shadows against the ground. It is on such a lazy afternoon that Zelunjo, the famous hunter of Ekwe village, finds us.

He is somewhere in the middle of the Old Forest, lowering himself onto his right knee, his Dane gun aimed at an antelope he could see amidst a thicket, one eye tightly shut and his nerves getting ready to squeeze the trigger, when our shrill cry tears through the stillness of the forest. The animal is startled into flight. Half-disappointed and half-curious, he follows our voice and ends up at an area of sparse vegetation under an Iroko. There, he finds a woman, naked from the waist down, still as a rock. In between her legs lay us, pink and bloodied, hands and feet striking the air, a slit between our thighs. Looking intently at the woman, the gloomy charcoal-black of her skin, her long matted hair, the sadness dragging her eyes deep into their sockets, the embossed scar coursing around her left ear, Zelunjo realizes that she is familiar. He recalls his countless visits many years ago to Umuaka River, at whose bank she'd lived. He'd watched her draw water from the stream and dry clothes by a hut. He'd hidden behind a tree, sometimes, and watched with pleasure as she washed her body.

Now, she is dead. In the Old Forest. With a child.

With *us*.

It is the way of Gods. When we decide to take up flesh, when a whole experience spanning centuries is squeezed into a human cage, we dissipate too much energy like a bullet in motion, such that as soon as we are born, the vessel is destroyed.

It is the price you must pay to carry the weight of time and timeless spirits in your belly.

It is what it is!

Had he known, Zelunjo might not have done what he does in that forest. He slashes the cord that kept us linked to the other side, rips off a part of his cloth to wrap us in its warmth, and then takes us home to Ijem, his wife.

'I found this child crying in the bush,' he says to her.

'Which bush, Nna-anyi? Did you not go to Oke-Ofia again?'

'I did,' Zelunjo replies, hanging his gun on a tree branch driven halfway into a wall crack.

'I don't get it, Nna-anyi. Do you mean to say that a woman came to the Old Forest to push out this child?' Ijem says, peering into our face.

Us, we look up at her, at her bulging eyes, the swelling in her neck, the patch of black skin underneath her left eye, shaped like Africa but without the horn. Then we start to cry, and she rocks us.

'We have to take this child to the village chiefs so they can decide what to do with *it*.' We feel her spittle land on our forehead. We curse under our breath.

'I don't think we should hand the child over to anybody,' Zelunjo says, 'I think we should keep *her*.'

'Keep her? Nna-anyi, how can we keep a nameless child? A child whose birthplace is the Old Forest? Did you even recognize her mother? Is she even from Ekwe?'

Zelunjo let his lips fall on the sides. We would come to know that that was the way he looked when he told a lie. 'Ehm, no. I don't know her, and I doubt she would have come from our village. Perhaps she is a madwoman from the neighbouring village who somehow got pregnant and wandered into the forest. Who knows?'

'The more reason she should be handed over to the chiefs, Nna-anyi,' drums Ijem, her voice grating our well-developed ears. We are getting tired of the back and forth; we want a little rest. So, we stop crying and start to scream, hoping they'd stop arguing. But Ijem does not get the memo. She rocks us even harder, draws us closer to her bosom, against the softness of her breasts, but continues to rant.

'How does anyone of child-bearing age not know it is taboo for a woman to step foot in the Old Forest? How does one not know that it is called the Evil Forest for a reason, the burial ground of outlaws, the belly that swallows blood sacrifices, the boundary between the freeborn of Ekwe and the outcasts of Umuosu. For all we know, this child could be an Osu, and we cannot—'

'Enough, woman,' Zelunjo snaps. We vibrate from Ijem's now trembling hands. 'Shut your mouth. You complain too much for a childless woman!'

We feel a pause in Ijem's heartbeat. A rush of shame and sadness. We hear her voice like it is from the back of her throat. 'I'm sorry, Nna-anyi. Please, let me bring you your food.'

'Better,' Zelunjo replies, easing himself into his armchair, 'I am the man of this house, and my decision is final.'

'Yes, Nna-anyi.' She curtsies, turns around, and walks head down into the kitchen.

Ijem is seated on the bench in front of her hut and squeezing cow milk into our hungry mouth when she tells Nkolika, her best friend who'd come visiting, how it all happened.

We are seven days old.

Ijem: I am not happy feeding another woman's child, Nkoli. A stranger's child, for that matter. I can't continue doing this.

Nkolika: Nne, this may be the gods answering your prayers. You have cried day and night for a child. Even as it might not have come from your own womb, this might just be the destiny Chukwu-okike has carved out for you. I think you should take this child as your own, Ijem. You never can tell, the gods might see you fit for motherhood through your actions and give you your own child.'

Ijem: My *sistah*, how can this be my destiny, *biko nu*? How do the gods give me a present wrapped in dirt? Eh? Why am I unable to keep my husband's seeds? Why does my womb keep throwing out children too early in murky blood?

Nkolika: Take it easy, *inugo*? Take it easy on yourself. What if the fault is not yours? What if your husband is the problem?

Ijem: Ah! Nkoli, please come and be going before you put me in trouble. The walls have ears. If my husband sends me away, I have no place to go. *Biko*, *bia lawa*, before you drag my feet to the village square. Have you ever heard that a man is *the* problem?

All the while, we are distracted by the milk in our mouth, smooth but a little sour. We like it; it is much better than what we are used to on the other side.

Also, we don't pay too much mind to their conversation. What is the point if we can't react? Our spirit has left the body and is out with Zelunjo as he meets with Ezemmuo, the chief priest. It is going to be the deciding moment. Whether we would be raised under Zelunjo's roof or tossed back into the Old Forest, Ezemmuo, the so-called mouthpiece of the gods, would decide. We watch as Ezemmuo casts the cowries and stones on the ground, observing them absorbedly, searching for answers. We giggle when he rises to his feet and dances in a circle around the scatter. We examine him when he towers over Zelunjo and breathes down on him, his tired, lined face, the white circle around his left eye, and—when he draws his face into a lifeless grin—his oak-brown teeth. Finally, he fixes his gaze on Zelunjo's eyes like he wants to see through him, to see *us* where we are squatting in the base of his skull, and says, 'Silence cannot be misquoted. Today, the gods have nothing to say.'

And Zelunjo, having dreaded a 'no' from the gods, sighs with relief.

We win.

We always, always win. It is the way of Gods. Of those of us with one foot on the other side. Spirit beings. When we choose to leave our resting place for this chaotic world, we come prepared, armed to the teeth.

Nothing is a match for us, not the human flesh, not the human gods.

So, there are only two options: win or win.

Finish!

We are named Mma, which means beauty, and right under Zelunjo's roof and the dutiful eyes of Ijem, we bloom into our name.

At eleven, we are a delicate-featured little woman, thin of frame, with moderately sized feminine features, and more importantly, the defiance of our foremothers.

When we think nobody is looking, we sneak into the small bush that leads away from our backyard, scuttling through a tumbling footpath and ending up in the Old Forest.

Us, in a small woman, looking up and fascinated by the vast sheet of green canopying so close to the sky we think it hugs the clouds, chuckling to the orchestra of chirping, squeaking, buzzing, cooing, and snarling things, and wondering why humans would call this boundless beauty 'Evil Forest' and declare it an abomination to the womenfolk.

At fourteen, we meet a woman on our way to the Old Forest. An aged woman with a slight stoop who clutched a walking stick in one hand and a bush lamp in the other. We murmur a greeting and make to move on, but she calls us back, holds us by our shoulders in a feeble grip and squints at our face. Then suddenly, like one who's had an epiphany, she screams a name she thinks is ours: Kambili? Kambili! We are taken aback, confused. She frowns. 'Kambili,' she begins, 'has your own mother grown too old that you don't recognize her anymore?' her thin lips quivering as she speaks. We say we are not who she thinks we are, that we are Mma, daughter of Zelunjo of Ekwe village. Flustered, almost teary, she says, 'Ah! Is this how people resemble people? You are a reflection of Kambili, my daughter. Look at your nose.' She lifts her shaky hand and touches our face, 'You both must have been twins in the spirit world.'

At that moment, we feel a pulse run through our spine, a shiver. Then, as if nothing has happened, we regain composure and ask, 'Where is Kambili now?'

And she replies, 'No one knows, my child. No one.'

But we do. We know everything that crosses our path, even the most secret things. For instance, we know Ijem sneaks into Chief Uwa's backyard after the women's meeting and that she now carries his child.

We know where Zelunjo goes after every hunt, before returning home. That he cannot resist the beauty of Obiageli, an Osu woman, scarred generously on her forehead.

We know that the old woman is Somadina, our mother's mother, and because her blood runs through the flesh we inhabit and she has touched it, she knows us too.

And humans are not meant to know Gods, so we know what we must do.

It is Nkolika who brings the news to Ijem. She tramps into the compound as though she has come for a fight.

'Ijem! Ijem *o*! where is this woman?'

Ijem appears from the backyard carrying an unfinished basket in her hands, our spirit folded in between the weaves.

'Nkoli, *ogini n'eme*? What has happened this time?'

'My *sistah*,' Nkoli strikes her palms together, 'this is not a story you tell standing.' She reaches for Ijem's wrist and drags her to the bench. 'Do you remember the foul-smelling hag that lives in isolation at the other end of Umuaka river?'

Ijem places the unfinished bamboo basket on the floor, rolls her eyes upward, and bites a finger in search of a memory.

'*Haba*,' Nkolika says, 'how can you forget the Osu woman that was said to have killed her husband and swallowed her only daughter?'

'*O! O!* Somadina? Isn't that her name?'

'*Gbam*,' exclaimed Nkolika, slapping her palm on Ijem's lap. 'That is the witch. I heard that Amadioha has finally given her the death she deserves.'

'Eziokwu?' Ijem eyes widen, her arms now akimbo.

'I am telling you,' Nkolika replies. Then she leans into the space between them and continues in a lowered tone, 'In fact, those who saw her body say it was swollen all over like she was pumped full of air and her skin peeled like a fowl dipped in boiling water.'

Flitting from stave to stave, we argued among ourselves:

- *We should have left her with a little more dignity. The final appearance was unnecessary.*

- *That body is pure art. How do we visit a place and not make a scene?*

- *She was innocent. The least we could do was kill her with kindness.*

- *Iyasikwa! What next, we ask their permission before we snuff the life out of them?*

The women can't hear our chattering.

'Chai,' Ijem exclaims, stretching her legs and crossing them at the ankles. 'Finally, the dead have taken their pound of flesh. At least we can now breathe some fresh air. That woman smelled worse than a dead pig.'

They both laugh. We roll our eyes, leap to the rim of the basket, and hang from it.

'Aha! I hear her kindred are coming from Umuosu to take her body into the Evil Forest'

'As they should,' Ijem spat. 'I must warn Mma to remain indoors, and you must tell your children same. You know the eyes of a child must not behold the corpse of an osu.'

'Of course,' Nkolika nods, 'otherwise, they become osu themselves.'

'The gods forbid!' Ijem throws her right arm over her head and snaps at the ground. 'Our children will not be doomed to isolation and ostracism!'

'*Ise!*' Nkolika responds.

'Our children will claim titles and own lands; they will break kola nuts and pour libations as freeborn.'

'*Isee!*'

'And our children shall attend the assembly of freeborn; they will marry freeborn and give birth to freeborn!'

'*Iseee!*'

The air grows darker. The hens begin to roost, and the birds fly to their nests. Nkolika rises from where she sits and smacks the dust off her buttocks.

'*Ngwanu, Ijem,*' she says, 'I wanted to be the first to share the good news with you. Let me come and be going.'

She spread her face into a wicked beam and tapped Ijem's back.

'*Daalu rinne*, thank you very much.'

'You know you are always welcome. What of your husband, Zelunjo, is he around?'

'My *sistah*, are men ever around?' Ijem says, and the two women throw their heads back and laugh.

'The most important thing is that they come back to you. Send my greetings to him, *inugo?*'

'I will. Good night *o*.'

Ijem picks up the unfinished basket and heads back into the hut.

Us, we return to the flesh that is our home.

***

Many days after, Zelunjo returns from his usual hunting trip to learn that Ijem is now, finally, pregnant. It sends him into a fever of excitement. Especially because since Ijem, he has taken other wives but has had to send them away as they too could bear no fruits. But now, his very first wife has successfully nursed his seed into a protuberant belly. And of course, there is no question about whose child it is. A woman would not be foolish enough to seek extramarital pleasures, and more so, a barren woman. Infidelity is a man's thing, a man's world.

So, Zelunjo, as is not uncommon, takes Ijem to Ezemmuo to find out if the child will be a man or a woman. Ezemmuo reveals it is a small man, another hunter like him, and his excitement becomes even more frenzied. He throws a party with his umunna and ebiri. Cows are slaughtered. *Ofe nsala* and *ofe onugbu* are prepared. Palm wine is poured from gourd to gourd, and *us*, darting from place to place, we like the smell that hangs in the air.

Especially the smell of fresh palm wine.

In our past life, we were both Islam and homosexual, and we were stoned for the latter before we could commit the haram of alcohol consumption.

But now, tasting the air, we can understand why Zelunjo drinks too much. So much that he staggers home in the middle of that night and misses his way, ends up in our room and lies with us. And through the night, his body is pressed against ours, his manhood pushing into the gash in the body we live in.

Our spirit-being forcefully defiled.

When the gods want to kill a man, they first make him mad. And what greater act of madness is there than fucking a God?

We know he was drunk, but what is done is done. And what must be done has to be done. It is a difficult decision to make, no doubt, for Zelunjo loved us. He wanted us. So, we spend the next few days debating among ourselves what to do with him, to him.

But as you might imagine, there are rules. If broken once, they must not be broken twice.

So finally, we decide, and that morning, our spirits go to play *tempe-tempe* in the walls of Zelunjo's intestines so that he wakes with an angry belly ache. His tongue is as though he'd been fed *onugbu* in his sleep, bitter and nasty, and his eyes feel dragged. When he climbs over Ijem and out of the bamboo bed, it appears to him as though the walls of his house are dancing around in circles.

So, with an oil lamp lifted into the air, he makes a slow delicate walk to the kitchen. There, he starts a small fire and sets a pot of water upon the fire stones. Then, he moves to the small garden in the compound and plucks some *uziza* and *onugbu* leaves. He looks around for the Awolowo plant—they say it clears belly ache, *fiam*—but to no avail. So, he crushes the leaves into the boiling water, and with the addition of some *ogogoro* for extraction, the water turns deep green. He scoops several horns of the concoction and swallows them in loud gulps, twisting his face and baring his teeth. Then, he pours libation to Agwu Nsi, the god of health, and wishes his illness away.

Soon, we are tired of playing, and we return to the human flesh.

He feels better.

He calls out to Ijem to tell her that he is going hunting, at Amaeke Forest, and would be back before sunset. He is a man after all, and a small bellyache cannot keep him away from his life's work.

But on this day, Zelunjo does not return home.

The news spread like bush fire in harmattan: Zelunjo, who had been hunting since his mates latched onto their mothers' breasts, who had moved quickly from using a catapult to kill lizards and squirrels to bringing home huge bush meats, who was the first to kill a leopard in the entirety of Awo community, went hunting in Amaeke Forest (not even the Old Forest) and did not come back.

By first light the next day, a search party is sent to Amaeke Forest, but after three days and three nights, the men return defeated. There is no information about his whereabouts.

And when Ezemmuo is consulted, he strikes his cowry-laden staff into the earth, and as it rattles, he does a small dance and says, 'A goat that dies in a barn was never killed by hunger.'

Our spirits, stretched to occupy the animal skin floor mat, listen. And through the fibres, we watch Ezemmuo dance away, incantations falling off his lips and tickling our ears.

The words are funny. We snicker.

In the days that follow, a dark cloak of grief shrouds Zelunjo's compound and spills into the rest of the village, enveloping every man, woman, and child.

We feel a bit of remorse, of course, sprinkled with sadness; this human flesh cannot be helped sometimes. And Ijem has become a sad-faced woman dressed in black, with a rapidly growing stomach and a bizarre craving for *nzu*.

Amidst her grief, she is believed to be unclean, able to contaminate others including herself. She is given a stick to scratch her skin should she itch. She is forbidden to speak to anyone but her fellow widows, and after her husband's body is buried, she will be interrogated by the Umuada over her husband's death. Her head will be shaved clean so that it gleams in sunlight, and her hands will be washed four times with *ujiji* to absolve her from her husband's death.

It is not easy for widowed women here. We still wonder how

humans forge these cultures that treat women so badly. It is not so on the other side. There, the creator is a woman, and she holds the world under her pedicured feet.

But in all of this, Nkolika never leaves Ijem's side.

One day, after a lunch of boiled yam dipped in salted palm oil, Ijem says to Nkolika, 'I had a dream last night, and in it, my husband died in the Old Forest.'

This time, we are latching onto Ijem's cornrows, eavesdropping.

'Ah, Ijem, you have come again. Did you not say Zelunjo went hunting in Amaeke Forest?'

'He did. He told me he did, but in my dream, his body was found in the Old Forest.'

She swatted a fly that buzzed around her ear and continued in a loud whisper, 'Mma was there too. There was a scar around her ear as though she were an Osu, and there was blood on her hands.'

'What are you trying to say, Ijem? Are you sure it is not the grief showing you things? Or a night fever?'

'I don't know, Nkoli,' Ijem confessed. She drew in phlegm from the back of her throat and lobbed out the sputum with a loud plop. 'But it seemed so real. So believable. Especially when it has to do with a child who could not come into this world without taking her mother's life, in the same forest.'

'I see.' Nkolika nods.

'And remember what Ezemmuo said,' continues Ijem, 'the goat that dies in a barn—'

Having received the signal we'd been waiting for, we leave Ijem's hair and crawl back into the body of Mma as she slept.

We are ready.

We know we went too far, but we had no choice. Rules are rules. We had been tainted by mortality, and all we had left in our power to do was damage control. We would be destroyed nonetheless!

So, we didn't mind using his nostril as a portal to his brain, to lead him instead to the Old Forest, where it all began, where it was going to end.

And we did.

Ijem was right.

So you see, sometimes, Gods are angels. But sometimes too, Gods are monsters.

At sunrise, Ijem will come to wake us up because we will take too long to wake; the water won't fetch itself nor the compound sweep itself.

But she will knock, and the door will not be opened. She will ask, and she will not receive. She will seek, and she will not find.

Because we would have returned to the beginning of everything. To a swelling void so dark, so deep, we will be nowhere and everywhere at once, just like the Gods that we are, always were, and forever will be.

Amen.

KALILOZE
Bwanga Kapumpa

The *sikuyeti* clutched his goat scrotum bag and shifted his weight again to get comfortable, the lucky beans and other charms inside it making beady noises. The locomotive he was on was old, its oil smelled ancient, and its rusty parts rumbled as the coal engine lumbered onward. Though the train's labouring motion could be heard within the booths, its noise was loudest in the open cars that contained a shipment of timber, where the sikuyeti sat.

While the railway lines and locomotives had been a welcome development, like many of the gifts from the white man, the people of the soil were not allowed to really enjoy their benefits. The people shared their land, but they were treated like the dirt they tilled. The ones that could afford a seat in the dilapidated cars reserved for black people made their journeys in some semblance of comfort. But the witch doctor superior could not afford a ticket to sit within the belly of the metallic, smoke-breathing snake. He could not read, but a worker at the train station informed him that the scrawls on the back of the ticket stub declared that the sikuyeti was boarding the shipment car at his own risk, that the Rhodesian Railway Company was not liable for any loss of life. Many people had fallen off the open wagon and perished, but a sikuyeti feared nothing.

The journey was long, but this was the fastest way to travel and get as close as possible to the river. More instant means of transportation existed, but they involved the dark arts of those the sikuyeti had sworn to kill. The witch doctor taps from the same mystical wellspring that the *muloi* or witch does. The difference between them is said to be their intention. While the witch doctor sought to heal, the muloi sought to kill. The sikuyeti made a lot of sacrifices to reach the level of witch doctor superior, but he was always reluctant about sinking further into the pit of darkness.

The train screamed and coughed smoke from its head. The sikuyeti shifted in his uncomfortable seat again. The ride did not bother him too much; he had experienced worse inconveniences. He was driven by a sole goal: to find and retrieve his *kaliloze* at the bottom of the Zambezi River. A kaliloze night gun is created by combining human bone and wood. While decorative elements like beads, lucky beans, cowries, and tree bark cordage may adorn and bind them, the weapon's base parts are bone and wood—a symbol of the close ties between man and the earth in the cycle of life. Its butt or handle is meticulously carved from the wood of a stretcher that was once used to cradle a corpse on its way to the grave, and to imbue it with more power, the barrel of the gun is from the femur of the deceased carried on the stretcher.

Kalilozes are as unique as their wielders, embodying the traits of its owner. It is believed that only initiated doctors or gunmen can use them; they cannot be used by laymen. Witchdoctor superiors seek out witches and use their guns to remove the threat. A family or the loved one of an afflicted person seeks a diviner who ascertains whether the cause of sickness or death is the malice of a muloi. The diviner then calls in or recommends a trusted sikuyeti. The name of the muloi need not be known; the kaliloze missiles are selective and seek out the offending witch across long distances.

Sometimes the night gun is used during the day and fired at

the rising sun because witches are said to congregate around the celestial sphere. An incantation is recited before firing:

Before the sun sets, the witch responsible shall fall and die from this retribution.

A year ago, the witch doctor superior retired. When he disposed of his weapon in the Zambezi River, he had hoped it would be the last time he would ever have to hold it. But danger was looming. He could *feel* it. It came to him like the smell of the rain before a downpour, a static current galvanising all practitioners in Barotseland. Cocks crowed at odd hours more frequently, and the ancestors whispered warnings but would not say what was coming. He would need his night gun.

He packed his goat bag with necessities and left his new home in Kalomo by locomotive to Mulobezi. There he would trek on foot for days to Senanga, through dense forest and thicket, and then make his way to the Zambezi, where he had gotten rid of his gun. He had moved to Kalomo in the south with the hope of beginning anew. The clusters of mud-walled huts and dusty terrain were nothing special, but they reminded him of Kalabo, his true home. He had not told his daughter where he was going when he left her there. *She is now a woman*, he figured. *She will find someone to marry.*

When the train came to a stop, the sikuyeti was still shaking from the journey. One of the other passengers sitting atop the timber haulage with him was also shaking from fear. The man had been drinking during the last leg of the train ride and had gotten inebriated. 'I find that a little drink makes these voyages less painful,' he had said to the sikuyeti in Tonga. The witch doctor superior only grunted in response. The man made more attempts at small talk but soon realised that the sikuyeti was not one for conversation. By the time night fell, the man was fast asleep. The sikuyeti fidgeted on his timber seat and wondered how anyone could sleep in such conditions. It was not long before the man leaned too far backwards and tipped over the edge of the car, gravity and terror yanking him from his stupor. When he opened his eyes again, the man realised that he had not fallen over and that the sikuyeti had grabbed his shirt. He slowly sunk back to his original position, and the sikuyeti returned to his. 'Thank you,' he whispered, his voice barely audible over the snake's metallic screech as it came to a halt. The witch doctor superior grunted.

Mulobezi was quiet that night. The passengers disembarked from the locomotive like life offered them nothing to be in haste for. Among them were a few Europeans, most of them haulage men from the British South Africa Company; even fewer were the people of the soil, most of them workers from the south. The sikuyeti wondered why the trainmen could not offer him and the drunk fellow more comfortable seats inside the booths if the snake's belly was barely full. He wondered why white men were so opposed to sharing the same space as his people. Of course, their ways and culture were different, but did they not all breathe the same air? Did they not eat when hungry, defecate when full, and bleed red blood when cut? Perhaps white men felt the same way about the people as he did about witches. Or perhaps, with their machine snakes and disdain for the people of the soil, the white men were witches themselves.

The sikuyeti stretched his limbs, and his whole body grieved. The train journey was long, but the trek to Senanga would be even longer. He asked one of the workers for some water and ate the boiled sweet potatoes he carried in his larger bag for supper. Afterwards, he walked to the farthest end of the train yard, where he found some vagabonds asleep under a shelter. He removed the wrap around his waist, balled it up into a pillow, and rested his head on it. He had a dreamless night.

***

Walking has a way of bringing a man's innermost thoughts to the fore. The longer a man walks, the longer he spends with himself, and his demons. The sikuyeti's feet and legs were not as lithe as they once were, so he walked slower than he would have liked. The rains would begin after the next full moon, which meant that the *Litunga* would be leaving his palace in the Barotseland floodplains for the one in the highlands, which meant that the witch doctor supreme would not have seen his daughter for a year. The thought troubled him.

Liseli was a bright young girl. When she was younger, the sikuyeti would come home from tilling the land to find her chasing his chickens around the compound or playing games with the other girls in the village. She harboured so much anger after her mother left, so much that when he came home, he would find her tormenting his chickens or fighting with the village boys. He always felt that she had inherited her mother's charm and visage, and his wrath. It did not help that the young ones teased Liseli because her father was a witch doctor.

He smiled to himself when he thought about her encounter with Mubita, the tallest girl in the village. Mubita had a disdain for chores and a penchant for stealing the clay pots of younger children as they walked home from drawing water at the well. Whenever any of the children confronted her, they earned a swollen lip and a mouth full of blood. The adults were afraid of her too because she had a venomous tongue and told many lies. Broaching the subject of her delinquent daughter with Mubita's mother was even more uncomfortable because she knew all the village secrets and would cause a scene when confronted. One day Mubita saw Liseli walking home with a bundle of firewood from the bush and decided to take it for herself.

'You can have it,' Liseli said, 'I like my lip the way it is'.

But before Mubita could walk away with her bounty, Liseli asked, 'Do you remember Muyangwa, the cripple?'

'Yes, I do. Before he disappeared, I often relieved him of his clay pot since he would spill half of its water before he got home anyway, owing to his hobble,' Mubita responded. 'Why?'

'He once tried to steal my clay pot, no doubt after running into you. I turned him into a field mouse. He had caught me on a very, *very* bad day.'

'Chicken shit!' Mubita retorted.

'Oh? See for yourself.'

Liseli produced a timid critter from the goatskin bag tied to her waist. She put it down, and it limped toward Mubita in an effort to escape. Mubita's heart beat like a war drum and threatened to free itself from her chest. Liseli looked directly into her bully's eyes, her face expressionless. Mubita placed the bundle of firewood on the ground and backed away slowly. She never crossed Liseli again.

The sikuyeti laughed until tears streamed down his cheeks when Liseli recounted the story to him. Of course, she did not possess the power to morph any person into a field mouse or anything else. Muyangwa and his mother had moved to a faraway village long ago in the dead of night, and not even Mubita's mother knew this. The mouse had been a victim of Liseli's rage, and when guilt consumed her, she had kept it to nurse it back to good health.

'I want to be like you,' Liseli told her father. 'I want to command the fear and respect that you do.'

But that was not the life the sikuyeti wanted for his daughter. It was not the vocation the ancestors had chosen for her either, even though he could have still passed on enough of his knowledge to groom her into a powerful practitioner. He reprimanded her often for touching his tools and suggested she learnt the ways of the white men so that she could outsmart them at their own game.

***

When the sikuyeti finally reached the banks of the Zambezi River, it was dusk, and several fishermen were preparing to go catch their food. The waves tapped the sand with a fondness, and the waters were calm. The men checked their lanterns and nets as they did each evening and then shoved their vessels into the Zambezi.

The witch doctor superior needed a canoe to get to where he had thrown his kaliloze but had no money to pay the fishermen. His many attempts to peddle charms yielded nothing, until a man with a leaky dugout canoe approached him.

'I overheard your conversation with the other fishermen and wondered if you had something for my manhood,' he whispered. 'I recently married a third wife. She is young and the only one who is frank enough to tell me that I am small and cannot satisfy her. Would you happen to have something that could help me?'

'As a matter of fact, I do,' replied the sikuyeti as he rummaged through his goat scrotum satchel. He produced an oddly shaped seed and handed it to the fisherman. 'Go and plant this somewhere no one will see, and water it only by urinating on it. As it grows, so will your manhood. When it reaches the desired size, uproot the seedling, pound it, and consume it with your morning porridge. I only require your canoe for the night and will return it early tomorrow morning.' With that, the fisherman handed him a calabash cut in half to empty the leaky dugout. He was about to give him a fishing net when the witch doctor supreme waved his hand. 'What I am fishing for does not require a net,' he said, and thanked the man.

The river had no landmarks or familiar indicators to guide the sikuyeti's journey; a lesser man would have gotten lost in the still night. But one needed memory as sharp as the bone-dagger he carried to become a witchdoctor superior. It also helped that he could feel his kaliloze call out to him. The call was not loud or even audible; it was more of an instinctual resonance. Like the feeling one got when being watched. He rowed the canoe slowly, his entire body still complaining about the journey it took to get there. He would occasionally pause to rest and empty gourdfuls of water that had seeped into the boat. Some restful sleep would have been a blessing, but it would be at the risk of slumbering forever on the riverbed.

When he got to the point where the call felt strongest, the sikuyeti anchored the canoe and emptied the water that had seeped in one last time. He said a prayer to his ancestors and dove towards the river's bottom.

Whenever he came up for air, each breath he took seemed colder than the last, each inhalation piercing his nostrils and chest. It did not help that he was exhausted and running out of air faster each time he dove into the cold, black water. But he feared that his fate would be much worse than drowning if he did not find his gun.

Realising that he could be taking his last breath, he dove as deep as he could, trying to drown out the voice in his head that was telling him that he would sink. His arms felt like solid rock, heavy with each stroke as he submerged himself further into the depths of the water. He could barely see his hands as he swam; how would he see his kaliloze at the bottom of this black basin? His only consolation was that he could still feel it calling out to him.

Water rushed into his ears, and that voice of doubt became even louder. His body felt like it would betray him; he yearned for nothing but air in his lungs. Just as he was about to lose hope, he saw a foreign object on the riverbed. There was no mistaking it; it was the bone-barrel of his night gun. The confirmation injected him with a wisp of vigour, enough to swim further down. He dislodged the kaliloze's stock from the wet earth. Another wisp of vigour. It was increasingly difficult to hold his breath, but reuniting with his enchanted weapon should be enough to power his ascent.

It was then that a muloi's sharp nails sunk into his right shoulder. He let out an inaudible scream, instinct quickly reminding him not to breathe. Blood poured out of the puncture wounds in his shoulder and began to blend with the near-black water. The sikuyeti could barely see and was still struggling to hold his breath. The voice in his head was relentless. *This is where you die*, it said.

The witch that had pierced his skin possessed the strength of a crocodile. She locked her legs around his knees and drew his back to her chest with her long arms. Barrel roll after barrel roll, there was no mistaking her reptilian resolve to kill the sikuyeti. His light was beginning to fade. *This is where you die*. He closed his eyes as the two bodies descended into what would be his resting place.

No. Not today.

He reached for the bone-dagger he kept by his waist and wriggled his arm just loose enough to stab at the wench locked on his back. It was not enough to mortally wound her, but it loosened her vice-grip enough for him to tap into the embers of strength he had left to break free. In one swift motion, he kicked her hard in the gut and used her as a springboard to dive down to his *kaliloze*.

When he picked up the weapon and whipped his body to face the witch, she was gone.

BOLD AS LOVE
Jocelyn Fryer

She rubs the owl pendant hanging on the front door between her fingers. A bright red door. The façade a welcoming sage green. The black bejewelled eyes of the tarnished brass owl stare back at her blankly. Or maybe beady, knowing. Mercurial, they tease her. This she takes as a good omen. She likes owls. She thinks back on a memory she has told no one, when, as a teenager, sneaking a menthol cigarette in her grandparents' home, in the French window of her dusty pink bedroom that overlooked the void of night sky with only a single glowing streetlight below, the pale owl that flew at her, wings spread a metre across surely, that scared the shit out of her, left her gasping for air, choking on minty smoke, before veering back into the darkness, the stars no more than pinpricks in the black fabric of the bewitching hour. Elvis Costello playing softly on her tape deck in the background, as if it had all been nought but a hallucination, bringing her abruptly back to normal, taking another pull on her menthol cigarette, her sanity reeling. Returning, she spots two Knysna Turacos in a nearby milkwood. Another good omen. Their plumage a vibrant green. Bright red wing-tipped, like the door, but velveteen. Their proud crests. Whenever she spots them in the wild, she is surprised that they seem bigger than she last imagined. The older she grows, the closer she nears thirty, the more she has come to quietly worship fowls of flight. Yes, this place will do nicely to build a life anew. Post-break-up. The price was right when it came to the monthly rental and deposit, and it was the only place she could afford that allowed pets. She would never abandon her cat to another. A stray that, more than anything or anyone in her youngish but steadily maturing life, has taught her the true meaning of loyalty. Of love. They belong to each other. And here, surrounded by so much natural innocence, they shall thrive, both her and the cat, she is convinced. Inside, the walls are a sandy brown. The built-in cupboards, baby poo. She envisages them, in her mind's eye, painted in a myriad of shades and hues of green. Green, green, green. She takes note of the big clock on the wall, faux country style with Roman numerals, all alone amidst the emptiness. She likes clocks. All timepieces, really. Watches and clocks. They reveal so much of a person. Speak volumes of a space. This keepsake of the tenants that came before. Obviously not treasured enough to take it with them. But she will prize it. In this home. A final good omen. The cottage itself is small but comfortable, with all the basic amenities. Not that she needs much. And at least it won't seem too bare, being so snug, with the little furniture she has left to her name. Yes, she consoles herself again; this place will do nicely.

The ward is blank. White walls. White linen. White uniforms. Punctuated only by the constant glare and buzz of fluorescent lighting. No clock to be found. All phones confiscated. Men sleep to the one side, women to the other. Before sleep comes to them, before the nurses snuff out their flame with their nightly medication, the men pace. Up and down. Up and down. Up and down the length of the ward. She buries her nose further into her book. She cannot bear such cruelty. The ceaseless pacing. She thinks of a wild cat sanctuary she visited with her ex once, where the lynx paced up and down the length of his long narrow cage. No, she cannot bear such cruelty.

The heartbreak has been harder than she had at first reckoned. Life alone in this cottage in the middle of nature, lush and verdant as it is, a mild soothing balm to the soul that is weary. Soothing, sure, but no miracle cure. Where at first she had felt a feeling close to relief, now the tears stream down her face when she is alone, to her thoughts, to her feelings. She longs for the love she has lost and is thankful, at least, for the companionship of her cat. And for the songs of the birdlife all around. It helps that her days, and nights, are mostly busy, too busy to waste on tears. Tears arise only in the rare in-between hours. Those in-between hours when she is carefully and meticulously folding napkins, patting them down, and smearing butter into ramekins for the tables at her job, polishing cutlery, setting up for the arrival of the rest of the staff. Those in-between hours when she lays exhausted in bed. Those in-between hours when she wakes and sips on her first coffee, then two, then three. Exhausted still, from tears spilled. But when she is helping her father with his failing restaurant by day, or working at her managerial job at yet another restaurant by night, and when the customers finally begin to roll in, life keeps her too busy for tears. Busy, busy, busy. It gives her some respite. Of course, the work on her masters has fallen to the wayside. She needs to write more pages per day, her supervisor tells her. And yet her concentration, when it comes to the analytical creature she used to be, now fails her. She wishes for the heartache to leave her be. At least a part of her does. But it clings, like a desperate infant, to her breast. Feeding on her. Rendering her sore and sick and tired. And she nurtures it, at least a part of her anyway. This ache, this grief. For it is all she has left of the love she had.

He calls to her from the solitary cell, from the restraints, calling her name over and over, calling for help, calling for salvation. Crying out. She wants to tell him there is no salvation here. This is the land that time forgot. The land where God came to die. God has been snuffed out with their nightly medication, just like their spirits, their fight. Pleas wasted. No blessed candles. Snuffed. She won't tell him this. Instead, she begs the nurse. Please may she go inside the locked room, to her friend restrained, and read to him from the Green Book of Fairytales. The nurse permits it but soon calls her back. Time for bedtime. But what has become of time? Punctuated only by the constant glare and buzz of the fluorescent lighting, in this land that time abandoned.

Every Sunday, up the road from her, there is a market on a plot of outstretched lawn. A plot that is, by the week, a dog training school. On Sundays, it comes alive with vendors of all sorts. And live music. Mostly crowd-pleasing, like Jack Johnson. It is the height of summer, just the right sort of weather for a market. She likes, too, to support the locals who grow and supply herbs and vegetables, rather than the larger chain stores. So soulless. And it is not far to walk to. These days, she prefers to walk where she can. The sun seems brighter, and brighter, with each passing day, and driving is too disorientating in the brightness. Walking suits her just fine. She surveys the market, taking it all in. She heads first to a van selling fresh oysters. She orders two. They are handsomely presented, in a neat bamboo paper boat, with a little two-pronged wooden fork. She adds a dash of green Tabasco and a squeeze of lemon juice and makes quick work of them, relishing how they smack of the ocean, these briny delights. Unadulterated. Pure. Oysters for breakfast. When her ex had always insisted spending hard-earned money on good food was a waste. So what? In this, she is finally taking a stand. She feels positively decadent. Deliciously self-indulgent. She browses amongst the stalls without much catching her eye. She picks up some tomatoes, onions, and a bunch of thyme from a young couple manning a stall of their garden's fruitful produce. A jewellery stall next draws her attention. She adores bespoke jewellery. And there it is. Magpie. A large oval stone, roughly cut, a seafoam green gemstone, set in silver. Seafoam green. Her favourite colour. A nourishing colour to her. Unadulterated.

Pure. Of the ocean, like the oysters. It isn't polished smooth like the other stones on display. It's rough like sandpaper. Raspy like a cat's tongue. And it catches the light with an incandescent glimmering. Its light is inside out, unlike the others. The jeweller, a young blonde girl sitting behind the display table, tells her that it is a moonstone. She slips it onto her left middle finger. It is a perfect fit. This time there is no longer any boyfriend to tell her what she should and shouldn't like. This time it is only her and herself alone to decide. With oysters for breakfast. And she has never wanted anything more than this ring. Or so it feels right then. She dishes out the cash for it, coveting it quickly, lest it be lost to a moment's hesitation and snapped up by someone else. It reminds her of a mood ring she treasured as a child. She twists it back and forth in the sunlight, swooning in its sparkle. And she feels stronger. Stronger than she has felt in some time. As if, for once, there is some universal thread at work in her life, beckoning her on to better things. Walking home, onions and tomatoes and thyme in hand, she continues to strengthen in resolve as if the ring might just be mystical. A holy stone. From it, she seems to draw a power, that she is a part of something so much greater. A cosmic kismet. She chides herself for such a fanciful thought. But then, yet again, it hits her like a wave. The splendour in things. The splendour in herself. And she walks, now in strides. The tarmac springy beneath her footsteps. Homeward bound. She bemoans her shoes, longing to be barefoot. Soon, soon. To the cottage she is coming to love. To a life she will learn to love in time. As her complimentary clock on a wall in the lounge tick-tocks away, in distant time to her strides. Tick tock. Tick tock. In time, in time, in time.

They are disturbed from slumber early, to shower. It is the only time she glimpses a dark sky from a barred window high above. They line up. Naked. The nurse she doesn't care for barks at them, 'Next, next!' and 'Hurry up!' as they shower three at a time. The girl who does not like to be touched elbows her in the tit in the shower. 'Get back in there,' the nurse barks again. Pressing herself against the shower wall to wash, lest she takes another hit, she does her best to rinse the soap off herself. Father, forgive me. Before they are all marched back to the room punctuated only by the constant glare and buzz of the fluorescent lighting. No clock.

She sits cross-legged on a picnic blanket spread out beneath the shade of a tree in her garden. She knows not the name of the tree, but she is charmed by its pretty blossoms. It stands so upright and proud. And so rooted. She takes it all in from her vantage point below, the outstretched boughs of the tree, the faultless blue sky with only the occasional white wisp of a cloud, one hand stroking her dozing feline beside her. Then, suddenly, she sees it. A small green snake weaving its way amongst the higher branches. For one fleeting instant, she feels her chest tighten. As a child she'd had a recurring nightmare of always swimming merrily in a pool of water, only to find herself surrounded by snakes, treading water, treading water, trapped. But curiosity gets the better of her. There is nothing particularly frightening about the creature. Not really. In fact, it is almost elegant even. She continues to watch it slowly make its way through the tree branches. Until, as suddenly as it appeared to her, it vanishes. She blinked, turned to look at the purring cat, and now it is gone, lost to her sight. She sighs to herself, dismayed. She thinks back on her recurring nightmare. She'd looked up the meaning of snakes in a dream book of symbols she had found in the library years later, and it claimed that such dreams were sexual in nature. But she was so very young. The pool of water ever-present in her nightmares needed no explaining. From the age of three, she'd been an incurable water baby, and be it a swimming pool or by the sea, her mother could never get her out of their depths. She dreamt of flying too when she was young. She would launch herself off her grandmother's French polished dining room table and fly, feeling weightless as in water. Another dream from her childhood comes to her while she gazes upwards, half-heartedly looking for the small green snake, still stroking the cat. In the dream she opens a door onto a diving board and a large swimming pool contained within four nearly endless walls. It is a long dive down to the water. But this doesn't concern her. She dives. Cartoon fish swim all around her, and they warn her that her mother is in danger. That she must save her from a terrible beast. Quickly she tries to climb the ladder railings back to the diving board, back to the open door, but once there, the other side of the door reveals a long corridor, and she is too late, a monster with fangs, carrying the limp corpse of her mother dripping blood, dripping, dripping, glides towards her. Then she wakes. Stealthily, she climbs into her mother's bed. She knows she is well past the age for such things. Recollecting now, she feels sorry for the child she was, so sensitive, so very afflicted by such horrors of the imagination. The small green snake remains hidden from sight. The sun is high in the sky, and she decides to retire indoors, calling the cat after her and shaking off the picnic blanket before folding it. She cracks open a cold beer from the fridge. Yes, she was a strange child. With so many imaginary friends. Real friends, other children, she had found, could be too unkind. She cared more for the snails in their garden and her trusty poodle than she did for the children at her school. Mean they could be. She remembers, too, birthday parties where she would tire of the other children and lock herself away in their pantry, instructing her mother to rid the house of the lot of them. And for the most part, her mother had indulged her. She muses on this as she takes another swig of her beer. She belches, downs the beer, and cracks open a second. It's her day off, after all. Day by day, she is growing less tearful, more resolute. Unconsciously, she fingers the moonstone ring and twirls it around and around. Her thoughts return to the snake in the tree. Momentary shock aside, she'd felt an overwhelming fondness for it. Like it belongs. In the same way that she and the cat belong here. And the clock that belongs, the clock that was there before them all, continues to tick away, its ticking hand soon muffled as she slots 'Bold as Love: The Axis by Jimi Hendrix' into

her grandfather's old stereo system. Unheard, the clock ticks all the same,
keeping time. 'Well, I'm bold, bold as love. Just ask the axis.'

She revolts. She refuses to eat anything other than ripened fruit.
Not this grey meal with sweet tea served up three times a day. If
only she could eat of the fruit of the tree sweetened by the sun,
fallen to the earth for eating, maybe then, its golden rays will soak
in, by proxy. How she misses the sun. How she misses her cat.
How she misses the birdsong. How she misses the ticking of the
clock. There is nought here but the constant glare and buzz of the
fluorescent lighting.

She is coming to know the lay of the land. The wildflowers that have
sprung up, yellow and purple. Wild garlic for cooking. Another a salve
for an itchy bite. Universe infinite. She has read that bees are most
attracted to yellow and purple flowers, and she marvels at the wonder
of nature as the yellow dandelions begin to flower all over, at the ready.
Their name means 'tooth of the lion'. She has recently looked it up.
Known for their bed-wetting properties if drunk in a brew. She knows
the creatures too. In her cottage, she has one gecko behind the geyser.
And another behind the clock. Until nightfall when the hunt begins.
She knows too the lone bumblebee that rests within a hole in the wooden
slat of her crooked fence. She has learnt too that they are industrious
pollinators, carrying a far greater load than the better-known honey
bee. Taking pity on the ants in her home, she has begun to leave them
little scraps from the table, on the kitchen sink, just for them, rather
than shun them, kill them. And she has never felt more alive and more
in perfect pitch, positively humming, with the greater harmony of all
living things. She feels a kinship to them that is close and intimate.
Soulmates. There is even a moth that visits her when the sun has retired
and the moon hangs heavy. The moth comes calling while she sits by
candlelight. She plays music for the moth. 'One Day' by Matisyahu

streaming on YouTube plays on a given night. She is spellbound as she watches its little antlers move furiously back and forth in time to the music. Antennae, really, but she prefers to call them antlers. It seems nobler. More fitting. More deserving. She does not name any of the creatures. They are not hers to name. They are simply the Beloveds. Watching the moth dance, she remembers a paper she once came across in her Honours year while researching for an essay on Cat's Eye by Margaret Atwood. She was visiting a friend at the time for a writing sabbatical, a friend who was busy with his master's in psychology. Both of them animals of the highest reason back then. Usually, they left each other while working, but this factoid was far too precious to wait for later. 'Hey, Ross,' she called to him. 'Get a load of this.' She read from the paper, 'Research suggests certain moths are drawn to Belladonna for the plant's hallucinogenic properties.' He chuckled. She chuckled. Moths get high? It comes back to her. She'd forgotten all about that day until now. 'Why,' she wonders aloud, 'would anyone want to bother with space, all the way out there, when there is so much right in our backyard? Eh, moth?' And by day, when she has time off, her masters relegated to the absolute margins, uncaring, she wanders around her little piece of land, collecting broken bits of china and seashells and sanded pieces of coloured glass to build a small cemetery where she lays fallen creatures to rest. Mostly geckos that her cat has tortured into an early grave. Anyway, that's life. With time, she comes to think of herself as a Roman Catholic cum Buddhist, whatever she thinks that means. First, do no harm, perhaps. Second, maybe, love boldly. Who can really say? All the same, she has begun to live by a certain creed of her own making. To be in blessed union with each and every creature, no matter how small, no matter how pestilent they are thought to be. To celebrate all in the garden, be it a herb she uses daily or a weed that serves its own divine purpose. This is her home, where she will do as she pleases. A kitchen overrun. Ants and all. A garden of its own making, wild and unfettered. Her working days are becoming increasingly frantic, her father's business near ruins, then rushing to her paying job where the restaurant is always fully booked, even turning tables. And yet, she returns home, to the place she loves most, amongst her kin, to find she has all the vigour in the world to wait up and watch the sunrise on a new day, to watch nature in all its magnificent guises unfold, this technicoloured tapestry. From the geckos that retire by daylight, to the daisies beneath the proud tree that gratefully unfurl at the first sign of sunshine. She loves, too, those unspoken hours from midnight until the birds are roused to song, as a dim mauve light begins to encroach. Colours have never been so vivid. Songs never so stirring. The sky never so endlessly expansive and all-encompassing. The moon. The stars. The sun. Her heart has never felt so full, so overjoyed, so perfectly attuned to the sheer magnitude of it all. Surely, surely, she grows ever certain, there must be a universal source for it all, for all of this, all living things so unspoiled in design. Designed just so. A higher wellspring from which all of this has flowed forth. Her mind boggles to think, but her gut tells her to believe. Or is it her soul? Believe, for it is so. And she has never believed more fervently. How else can it be? She reasons with herself, but logic fails her. Maybe her soul knows best, she counters, in the wee dark hours of the morning, before the birdsong comes to enflame her from such bargaining. The birdsong only confirms what she longs to be true. And so it is. While the clock that has been there the longer keeps ticking away. In time, in time, in time. 'Just ask the axis.'

The psychologist asks her if she knows what day it is. She erupts, laughing. Maniacally. She shouldn't. It is clear from his face that this is not the reaction he wants. But she thinks him mad. She is locked in the land that time forgot, that God forsook, with no windows, no clock to speak of, only the constant glare and buzz of the fluorescent lighting, and this man, in all seriousness, wants her to name the day of the week. Is this some bizarre test of her state of mind? For all she knows, it's been a day or a lifetime. She laughs still. Unable to stop. No doubt this will cost her, but she cares not anymore. He asks her more questions. No, she is not suicidal. No, she does not hear voices. But she thinks to herself, I shall never ever tell you of my cottage beloved by the universe, by God, by Buddha, and filled with Beloveds, of my wildling heart amongst all other wildlings. That is my secret to keep. And again, she laughs. And she laughs. And she laughs.

She cannot recall a day warmer than this. She runs her frock under a tap of cold water, wringing it out and wearing it to cool her. She cracks a cold beer, relishing the first sip. She selects some ska music from her collection and cranks it up. She dons her wide-brimmed summer hat. Ruefully, there is a moment where she thinks about her ex. He'd said that with her short hair, she looked like a cancer patient in a hat. 'But we don't care anymore, do we?' She holds her moonstone ring out to bear it aloft, haughtily, next ruffling the fur on the crown of her cat. Beer in one hand and picnic blanket in the other, she heads for the tree, some shade and some relief. She has learnt a new word recently for the filtered flecks of light beneath a tree. It is Japanese. Komorebi. She likes to collect words. Embodiments. It is the playful season, and the baby monkeys are out, bouncing up and down on the green netting hanging over the wooden poles of the carport. She watches them and dances gleefully with them in time to the music blaring in the background. Like a scene out of The Jungle Book. But soon she grows sweaty. It is simply too hot. She retires to the blanket and the cold beer waiting for her in a chilled silver tumbler she found as a set of four at the Sunday market. She'd once been told that drinking from silver had healing properties. Whether this was true or not, she frets not now. For now, as long as it keeps her beer chilled, she is content. Her wet frock clings to her skin, shielding her from the heatwave. But soon it is dry again. She goes inside to top up her silver tumbler. She stops by the bathroom, splashing her face with cold water. She returns outside, only to find that a breeze has begun to stir. The trees, the bushes, the flowers, they all seem to sway in the breeze in time to the ska music playing out on her stereo. In jest, she acts conductor, swaying her arms, gesturing with her hands. Please rain, please rain, please rain, she begs inwardly. And as if she called them into being, in the same way God uttered 'Let there be light,' heavy clouds begin to gather, sun shining all the while as droplets begin to fall, cooling the earth, cooling the cheeky devils bouncing on the green mesh, cooling her right down. A monkey's wedding. She sits there resplendent in the rain and the sunshine, not for once flinching or rushing indoors. Did she conjure the clouds? Were her prayers answered? Could you wish upon the universe as if it were a star or a coin in a fountain? And nature continues to dance to the music, the monkeys continue to play, and the phone begins to buzz. Endless message after the next. Concern. But she doesn't give a fuck. Right now she is the master of the fucking universe. Off goes the Wi-Fi device, off goes the phone. The ska continues to blare. But the clock that was there before stops. She must get a new battery for it; she makes a mental note, giving it a cursory glance as she grabs another beer. It is only later, when she relents and turns the Wi-Fi back on, that the clock begins to tick again. Surely, not. Surely, she imagined it. Or is the cottage, maybe, just maybe, truly at the very centre of it all, at the axis, as bold as bloody love? The cottage that could stop time. She ponders, more than a little, then takes a swig of her beer and belches. 'Well, I'm bold. Bold as love.'

She has emerged, four months later, not so long in a land that time forgot, in a land punctuated only by the constant glare and buzz of fluorescent lighting. Or maybe not. Maybe it was an eternity. All the same, here she is, released, on the farm plot of a dear friend of her mother's. Seeking refuge. She longs to find God again, or even a loosened thread of the grand universal tapestry, in the design of things, in the miraculous splendour. How long must she suffer? At four a.m., like clockwork, the rooster crows. She stretches and rises from sleep. She places the kettle on the gas stove. The birds break the dawn with their song. The recent litter of kittens are already pestering her cat, much to the cat's feigned irritation. But she knows the cat will grow to care for them in time. She trusts the cat will prove maternal after all. That she will nurture them. In time. She will soon begin work on her masters, on this fine morning. It has been of some comfort. To have something to sink her teeth into, as the saying goes. It is too hot to work in the Klein Karoo in the afternoon, and her mother's friend has told her a siesta is the order of the day. All is good. Mostly. But she longs for that fullness of her praising soul again. How long, again she wonders, will she have to wait before her supplications are answered? But it comes. Oh, it comes. As the sun begins to sink a little lower, she awakens from her siesta and leaves the cool of the cottage for the patio. The mountains, the trees, the bush, all are enshrined in a strange light, in a glorious orange haze, almost amber, like she has never seen before. She will ask her mother's friend about this strange light later, over dinner. 'There's a word for it. It's called gloaming,' her mother's friend will tell her. She will run the word over and over, rolling it up and down her tongue like a pebble, without uttering a sound. Over and over in her mind. Over and over in the depths of her soul. Gloaming. And she will be still, be still that beating heart, and know that it is God. In the land where time moves to the course of God's will. In roosters crowing, in sunrises and hellish afternoon heat, in shooting stars whizzing by beyond. And she will still her racing thoughts, still her bare soul. She will commune again. In gloaming. And in time, in time, in time. Everything in good time. Bold. Bold as love.

IN RHYTHM AND SPIRIT
Victor Ola-Matthew

Man is twenty-seven and different from you. Very different, peculiar. Different in the sense that he communicates with the dead for a living, as a gift, and for as long as he lives. His tiny apartment in Bariga is not that peculiar, however. It is a room and a parlour. Two rectangles is how he describes it. In his parlour (which also serves as his kitchen), he has carved out a place for work. A table and three stacked chairs. There are two calabashes, half-filled with a concoction of palm wine, a white cock's blood, and *agbo*. Both covered and trapping their smell. They are like Pandora's box. Never to be opened. At least, not yet.

For this workspace to exist, Man has a bean bag for a couch and no television—he does have Netflix on his phone. On the table are cowries, a Ouija board, a telephone whose wire is cut short and connects to nothing, a black pen, a jotter from Iya Salake Ajoke's burial (1935–2006, courtesy of her grandchildren), a hand-sized shard of broken mirror, and a Supa Strikas comic. Opposite the table, which sits at one end of the rectangle, are the kitchen, entrance, and exit. They are one door. It terrifies him. At the left of the table is the door to the other rectangle where he sleeps. The door is ajar, but now he thinks to close it as there is a knock on the entrance door. It must be Fawe, the jambite. He'd have to cook up an excuse why he cannot explain polynomials to her this afternoon as he is expecting a guest.

For Man, there is barely anything nice about afternoons, especially in March. The weather is hot, there are bills to pay, and there is an errant supply of electricity. There is also the constant existential crisis for one who sits at home and, worse, communicates with the dead. There is dust gathering on the floor, in the nets, in the fan, in the air. Vehicles and students pollute the already present but bearable noise. Is there ever some quiet on the roadside of Bariga? No. There is barely anything nice about afternoons but the woman at his door today. The woman who stands at the door is more than just nice; she is beautiful with a perfectly sculpted round face and glossed lips.

'Come in,' Man says. Man must now put on his best behaviour despite his unkempt dreads and the large sweat patches in the armpit and at the back of his yellow and black rugby shirt. He looks up at the ceiling fan, hoping that it comes alive. As if in communication with Man's spirit, the Power Holding Company restores electricity. The street roars, celebrating.

She is desperate. For answers, for help, for comfort. Her desperation is the vehicle that has brought her into the home of a man who looks mad. He smells. What is this cubicle he lives in? It smells. Woman must take off her Hermes sandals at the door. She must step on the grainy red rug with her barefoot, black handbag at her elbow, black turban hiding her black hair, black gown sweeping the ground. She must stare through her black sunshades at Man, who is now rushing to offer her a seat at the table. He pulls a chair out of the stack and, with a creepy grin, says, 'Please sit.'

Woman is crazy—she thinks so. Her sister says it's grief, but this is rather new. A new emotion, and grief is not her name. She would rather it be called emptiness because that is the feeling when you lose your perfect lover. And Woman, she longs to fill this emptiness with anything, with everything. She has worn all of her lover's clothes, slept by his graveside, worn his retainers for a week, and made ethereal love to him in her dreams. She has done it all, yet he ceases to exist but in flashbacks and memories. All she has done should mean something, or better still, do something. It should make him reappear in the flesh for a second, make the heavens and earth glitch and the ground spit out his black and gold coffin. Yet, nothing moves. The world has carried on as if someone somewhere has not just lost her lover. The roads are still busy, a building has just collapsed, a helicopter has just crashed, some hungry mourners and eyewitnesses are looting, a *buka* is getting filled, customers are dining, a woman is pounding, a man's palm wine has just tipped over, a mourner is mourning, a hawker is hawking, a pedestrian is crossing, King Sunny Ade is playing, Manchester United is losing, the climate is worsening, and rain is pouring while dead lover's woman is in his bed sniffing his Tuesday and Wednesday shirts, spraying the room with the last of his Arabian oud. At least she is here now. She has heard Man can communicate with the dead and intercede on her behalf, so she sits as he directs but sticks her legs to the side because of the calabashes under the table.

They introduce themselves. Man and Woman. Names are nothing but the identification of a person in the physical realm. Your real name is the name of the first man that has reincarnated over the centuries to become you.

'What brings you here?'

'I want to speak to my lover.'

He corrects her. He reminds her that she can always speak to her lover without his gift. She has come to hear what her lover has to say—if he has anything to say. Woman nods in agreement, and the ritual begins. He pushes the Ouija board, the jotter, and the pen to the side because, today, those will not be necessary. He puts one calabash on the table and asks for her hands. Woman obediently submits them, and he places them on either side of the calabash. He surrounds the calabash with cowries, placing two on the top and two on every side. The calabash is covered, burying its soon-to-be uncovered stench. Beneath his chairs is his brown *irukẹrẹ*—a fly whisk made from the hairs on the tail of a horse—which he whips out. Alas, he must open the calabash and stifle a laugh when the miasma of the rotten organic concoction sends Woman out of her chair. Too bad he must also sprinkle it on her with his *irukẹrẹ* when she returns to the chair. She truly is desperate.

Man asks that Woman resubmit her hands, but this time, she is hesitant as she is unsure what to expect. He puts hers in his. Hers are tender and warm and very shaky, unlike his, coarse and steady. She is nervous; he is in control. He begins to speak in a foreign tongue.

I call on the ocean. I call on the rivers.
I call on mother nature. I call on her sisters.
I call on the earth. I call on the trees.
I call on mother nature and her daughters that be.
I call on the sun. I call on the sky
I call on mother nature and her sons, most high.
I call on the grave. I call on the dead
Revive, revive, let your voices now come alive.

As his voice rises, Woman trembles within. Does Man know that the blacks of his eyes are no more? The concoction in the calabash no longer smells and begins to darken till it assumes the image of a void, a black hole.

'What was his name?' Man asks. She is still enthralled by what she sees: A man with no lens and pupils, just his reddish sclera. He asks again. 'Your lover, what was his name?'

She tells him. All of it. His first, last, and middle name. Even his alias. She says it all. He asks that she speak into the calabash and the blackness therein. She obeys, and immediately, the telephone connected to nothing begins to ring. He lets go and raises the handset from the cradle. He puts it up against his pointy, right ear. At first, there is static, then whispers. His lenses are back, and the concoction has returned to the organic rubbish it had always been. Her eyes light up.

'Speak. He is listening,' Man says to Woman.

She has waited weeks for this moment. She has done crazy things in her grief, hoping to cheat death, only to find her solution in the dusty streets of Bariga and be tongue-tied. She realises that she never really knew what she wanted to say to her dead lover all along.

'Tell him I miss him,' she says

'He says he misses you too.'

Woman smiles. Man tells her that her dead lover says he loves her dress, and she laughs aloud, trying not to be flattered but failing.

'I am mourning you,' she tells him—both of them.

Man says her dead lover says she shouldn't stop, that she is a beautiful mourner. He—the dead lover as she is told by Man—says that her eyes are beautiful today, that her skin is the finest of all roasted cocoa, that her lips, if only he could lay his fingers on them once more, not to talk of kissing them. Her dead lover tells her all these romantic things, and they make her laugh. They make her happy. They make her feel loved once more.

Woman asks where he is, and he, her dead lover, says, 'I cannot disclose.' He adds, 'You don't want the Feds to get me.' She laughs. Death has made her long-dead and buried lover so much funnier. He did not have much deliberate humour in him, but look at how death changes a man. She tells him that perhaps she should also die so she can fulfil her new dreams of becoming a stand-up comedian in the afterlife.

Her dead lover asks that she update him on everything he has missed, so she does. She tells him about how she has exhausted his

Arabian oud, about how he makes good love to her in her dreams, and about the terrible government. 'Thank goodness I am free from that crap,' her lover says. Take me with you, she jokingly pleads. She tells him about Omawunmi's album, 'Timeless', her growing love for jazz, and the book by Alice Walker, which she is currently reading, 'The Colour Purple'. They talk for an hour, then another, before she acknowledges that Man's hand must hurt from holding the handset against his ear. But even he seems to be enjoying her conversation with her dead lover. He sees her. He knows her secrets and romantic fantasies with her dead lover, but she is unbothered.

'We should end the call now,' she tells Man.

One who speaks with the dead does not await his inter-realm telephone to ring before he begins to hear things. Speaking with the dead is a costly gift, and it plagues you. Man does not have schizophrenia, yet when he bends in the market and looks between his legs, he sees spirits walking on their heads, singing, whistling, humming, possessing. As the sun is shining and rain is falling, spirits gather beneath rain clouds and dance to the sound of talking drums. Talking drums that beat as loud as thunder, yet no man born of flesh—and flesh alone—hears. Man is familiar with his plagues. Too familiar that his fear is not the plague itself, but the randomness of its manifestation. When he bathes, he hears knocks. Spirits are clamouring to be heard by him. They want to send him on errands, possess him, beg him to tell their wives one thing or the other. On days when there are no knocks, everything sounds like a knock because he is expecting one. Man is mad.

He hears his name after he closes the door behind Woman. The voice is not hers; he knows this. Still, he opens the door to confirm. Woman waves at him. Awkward. He hears his name again, and this time he recognises the voice. It is the voice of Woman's dead lover.

'How dare you?' he asks.

'How dare I *what*?'

Spirits are rude. Man is aware of this. They don't need verbal consent. Curiosity is enough of a key to open up all of yourself for them to come in. All you have to do is want to know, want to hear, want to see. Just want. Man wanted to hear what Woman's dead lover had to say, so he heard.

The conversations between a man and a spirit are not by word of mouth but can be if a man desires. They are neither of trance, or images, or possession, but can be if a man desires. Neither Man nor Woman's dead lover is *desiring* as they communicate. The world continues.

'Spare me your pretence. You dare lie in the name of the dead?'

'I am trying to help her. She looks miserable.'

'She is in mourning, you fool.'

'She is past mourning. She is obsessed with the idea of resurrecting you.'

He—Woman's dead lover—appears. Not out of nowhere. Out of the calabash on the table that remained open. How he looks, Man cannot describe. No one can. For all one knows, Man could be speaking to his gas cooker.

He accuses Man of not telling his lover all the things he had said—and the manner in which the words were spoken. Man did not tell his lover that he had asked her to forget about him, to move on. He did not tell her that her dead lover thought the turban did not suit her quite well. And he did not make any of the death jokes. 'Feds, really?' Woman's dead lover scoffs.

'Didn't you see the way she laughed? She was happy,' Man defended.

Woman's dead lover hissed. He called Man a corrupted fool who, for his lust, was lying in matters that concerned a dead man and his lover. 'Have you no fear?' he asks.

'No, you are forever dead.'

'I curse you.'

A knock follows, and it interrupts Man's conversation with his matchstick. How dare it not be spirits stampeding for his attention? How dare it not be Fawe with her New General Mathematics textbook on her head? How dare it be Woman at his doorstep sobbing?

'My lover is dead,' she comes in, crying.

Woman is crying on the chest of a stranger. A weird man who communicates with the dead for a living, but not as weird as the telephone now ringing. She backs away.

'The phone is ringing,' Woman points out.

'Look at that. It must be your lover.'

She doesn't wait for him to direct her before she sits comfortably in the chair like one familiar with Man and his tiny apartment. A few minutes back, when the door was shut behind her, she began to feel things as she made her way to her car. The things she felt, she could not name, but they overwhelmed her as soon as she got into her car. She burst into tears. It was emptiness once again. Nobody speaks of the day one's purpose is accomplished, how empty one feels because they know, soon, they will have to find another. Woman had achieved her burning purpose, and all she had left was the feeling of emptiness and the question, 'Is that it?'

'Is he still there?' she asks.

'Yes, you're lucky I have not severed the connection.' Man places the handset against his ear as he speaks with a broad smile.

'Why?' She is far too intrigued to return the smile.

He tells her that one cannot summon a spirit as they wish, that spirits could get offended when they perceive disrespect and demand blood as a remission. When he sees that she is alarmed, he laughs and tells her it is only a joke, although it is not.

Woman leans in. 'Does he hear everything we have to say?'

'No. He hears as much as you are willing to let him hear. Why do you ask?'

She shakes her head gently and replies, 'Nothing,' and much to her surprise, Man does not persist. Instead, he says, 'Might I get you anything to drink?' She declines, but he insists because he hears loud voices in his head. They are driving him crazy, but how does he explain this to her? He gets up and walks to his mini-fridge.

'I have malt,' he says. He doesn't hear her reply because her dead lover's voice is overwhelming. His voice fills Man's head, demanding that Man lets him in, declaring war against Man in a spiritual battle that Man is now losing. There are so many knocks on the door of his soul.

'What did you say?' Man asks Woman, standing over her with a can of malt in his hand.

'I said I don't drink malt,' she replies, collecting the can from him because he is handing it to her despite her refusal. Suddenly, it begins to rain although the sun is shining and Bariga is very hot. Through the window, it looks like a drizzle, yet it drums on the rooftop like hail. 'Oh, look at that, it is raining,' she says.

'Yes, who would have thought?' Man says absentmindedly. 'Do you remember how to tango?' he asks Woman.

She wants to ask him how he knows this fact about her, but because she could never resist an offer to tango, she responds with a scoff, 'Do I remember?'

'I fancy myself a challenge. Would you like to dance?' he asks, offering his right hand. 'Naughty Little Flea has always been your favourite.'

'But there isn't any music.'

'I'll sing.' And before she can say anymore, he lifts her to her feet. Woman almost crashes into Man, who begins to sing, his right arm wrapped around her waist and his left hand locked with her right. They dance, moving from a slow to a fast tempo, mimicking each other's steps with intense familiarity in rhythm and spirit as if they had tangoed together in the past, as if they were lovers in their past lives.

'Omebere,' Man calls.

'Richard.' Woman looks Man in his eyes. He has called her by the native name given to her by her grandmother. A name she has not disclosed to Man, a name only one man who no longer resides on the earth knows. 'Is it you?'

THE GOOD SHEPHERD
Efua Boadu

Police interview transcript: 002

DS Mayhew: Detective Sergeant Mayhew and Detective Johnson interviewing.

Please state your full name and occupation.

Jackson, C: Chris Jackson. Delany's Jam factory floor manager.

DS Mayhew: You've come to file a missing person's report, is that correct, Mr Jackson?

Jackson, C: Yes, that's right. The ladies on the floor made me call up. Is everything okay?

Det. Johnson: Please could you tell us what you know about Enid, Emmanuel, and Rachel Mutesi, Mr Jackson?

Jackson, C: I, I don't know much about them. Er, Enid's a good girl, a good worker.

She'd never take time off without telling me or any of the factory girls. She's worked at the factory for over ten years, and she's never taken any unauthorised leave, never. She even comes in with flu and that. Very hard working is Enid. That's why the girls have been fretting so much. It's not like her at all.

DS Mayhew: When was the last time you saw Mrs Mutesi, Mr Jackson?

Jackson, C: Just over a week ago. She didn't come to work last Monday.

DS Mayhew: And how did Mrs Mutesi seem to you the last day you saw her?

Jackson, C: Yeah, she seemed fine. I didn't speak to her that much. She's not a talker. Bit reserved, like. But she seemed her usual self. She's popular with the girls. There are quite a few Africans working at the factory. They're hard workers, the women, anyway. Enid's given me no trouble for as long as I've been at Delany's. You don't think anything's—

Det Johnson: Well, we don't know. It's early days, but I can tell you that a missing person's investigation has been launched. A bulletin went out yesterday. Any information you can provide on Mrs Mutesi and her family would be greatly appreciated. You say that Mrs Mutesi was popular at work? Could you give us a list of anyone that was close to her?

Jackson, C: Yep, sure. We're not a big company. I can give you a list of names, no problem. The girls will be cut up when I tell them. Enid and her family, missing? She's so quiet and . . . and religious. I'd never think of her getting into any trouble. Her husband's the same. I've met him a couple of times. Quiet chap, very well-mannered. He does stuff for their church. We've donated jam and pickles and stuff like that to their charity fundraisers. It's the only time she asks me for anything. Wouldn't say boo to a goose, would Enid. I really hope everything's alright. Would be such a shame, a shock even if—

DS Mayhew: Well, let's not jump the gun, Mr Jackson. Nine times out of ten, we find the missing persons safe and sound. Is there anything else you can tell us about the Mutesis?

Jackson, C: Er, they're from Uganda, that's it. I really hope nothing bad's happened.

Det. Johnson: Is there anything else you'd like to add?

Jackson, C: No, I think that's it. Sorry I can't be of more help. If there's anything me or the girls can do, just let us know.

DS Mayhew: Will do. Thank you for your time, Mr Jackson, you're free to go.

Interview terminated at 7:12 p.m.

Police interview transcript: 010

DS Mayhew: Detective Sergeant Mayhew and Detective Johnson interviewing.

Please state your full name and occupation.

Williams, P: Pastor Paul Williams. Pastor and founder of the Holy Spirit Redeemer's Church.

DS Mayhew: Mr—

Williams, P: Pastor, please, if you don't mind.

DS Mayhew: Sorry, Pastor Williams. Thank you for coming to see us again.

Williams, P: Of course, anything I can do to help. When a shepherd loses his sheep, he will do everything in his power to find them. How is the investigation progressing?

Det. Johnson: We're not at liberty to go into too much detail. It's still early days; we're following up a few different leads. We have some more follow-up questions if that's okay? According to information that we've received so far, you may have been one of the last people to see the Mutesi family.

Williams, P: Oh really?

Det. Johnson: Can you tell us once again how the Mutesi family appeared to you after your church service on the seventeenth of March?

Williams, P: Yes, they were in good spirits. Nothing unusual, as I previously stated. I greeted them, and we talked about the sermon; then they went off to chat with some other church members, and that was it. No, wait, I did speak to Emmanuel briefly about a few charity matters. We're holding a fundraiser soon, and I wanted to make sure that things were on-track.

DS Mayhew: Was Mr Mutesi working with anyone else on the fundraiser?

Williams, P: No, no. Just him and me. We are a small church. Emmanuel is an excellent organiser, so I leave it to him. He's very conscientious.

DS Mayhew: How did Mr Mutesi seem to you when you were discussing these plans?

Williams, P: Yes, fine. No stress. He's a very calm person. Devoted to God, clever, hard-working. We raise a few thousand pounds every year for the local community and for the maintenance of the church.

DS Mayhew: Is Mr Mutesi involved in any of the church's financial affairs?

Williams, P: No. I look after the church finances. I take care of the books, make sure that everything's running smoothly. The charity is linked to the church but is registered under a separate charitable entity.

DS Mayhew: And who looks after the charity's finances?

Williams, P: I do overall, and Emmanuel helps me. I pride myself on running everything in a Christ-like manner, irreproachable under the strictest scrutiny. I will be more than happy to share with you all the church and charity financials if you like?

DS Mayhew: Yes, that would be very helpful, thank you. I hope you understand, we have to examine all lines of enquiry.

Williams, P: Yes, I understand. The Mutesi family are one of the bedrocks of our congregation. It's not the same without them, and I can't tell you the amount of extra responsibilities I have to shoulder without Emmanuel's help.

Det. Johnson: Right. Could you tell us more about your personal relationship with Emmanuel and Enid Mutesi?

Williams, P: As I wrote in my statement, I have known them for about seven years, since I established the church. They were the first family to attend services. We, my wife and I, are close to the family. Emmanuel is in my office almost every day, giving me updates on charity initiatives, and of course, we see them every Tuesday, Friday, and Sunday for service. From time to time, they invite my wife and me for dinner along with some other members.

We all enjoy each other's company.

Det. Johnson: And did they ever speak to you of any problems they had? Financial, work-related, or personal?

Williams, P: Whatever my sheep tell me remains strictly confidential. I am not at liberty to speak of such things.

DS Mayhew: Mr, Pastor Williams. Can I remind you that this is an official police investigation? Do you want to help us find the Mutesis or not?

Williams, P: Yes, of course, I do! Please don't get the wrong idea. It's just that I feel uncomfortable divulging private confidences because they are just that, private. There wasn't anything major. They are a happy family, as far as I'm aware. Their only real worries were for the wellbeing of their families back home. Uganda is a very poor country, officers, and there are always school fees, medical bills, or a marriage or funeral to pay for. Emmanuel receives a modest income from the charity, and Enid also earns a modest amount at the factory.

DS Mayhew: So, they did have financial difficulties?

Williams, P: Money was tight, but that's the case for everyone in my church. We're Africans, poor people who work hard to make ends meet and rely on the grace of God.

Det. Johnson: What was their relationship like with their daughter, Rachel? Do you know?

Williams, P: Yes, yes, it was good. Excellent. Rachel was born around the time the church was established, and I know that they were very happy to be parents. Though Enid once told my wife that she wished to have more children. But so far, God has only blessed them with one child. Enid's a very good mother. She looks after the girl very well. And she's clever, Rachel. You can give her complicated sums, and she can work them all out in her head. Sharp as a razor blade—

Det. Johnson: I'll give you a moment.

Williams, P: It's fine, thank you. I just hope and pray that nothing serious has happened to them. According to you, they've not left the UK, though their car is missing, so they must be here somewhere you can find them, officers. We've been holding prayer vigils for them every night since the first time I came to see you.

Det. Johnson: I just want to take you back to what you said about Mrs Mutesi's desire to have more children. Did you say that she confided in your wife about this?

Williams, P: Yes. Women's things, so I never enquired into the details. Emmanuel never mentioned anything. He's a very proud father and loves Rachel very much. Please God,

please let them be okay.

DS Mayhew: Did Mrs Mutesi ever talk to you about any other worries?

Williams, P: No. The last discussion we had was on the subject of evil. She said that, at times, she felt like she was being outwitted by the devil. I was a little taken aback, as she's normally a positive person. I asked her to explain, but she was a little unclear. She spoke about the world around her and the evil she sees on the TV and the internet, things that we're all exposed to.

DS Mayhew: And what did you say?

Williams, P: I told her to limit her exposure to the news and internet and pray more, read the Bible, things like that.

DS Mayhew: And what was Mrs Mutesi's response?

Williams, P: She nodded. That was it.

DS Mayhew: How did she seem to you after the conversation?

Williams, P: Fine. She reflected for a moment, then she went to talk to my wife and some others, then they left.

DS Mayhew: Is there anything else at all that you can remember from any other conversation you've had with the Mutesi family recently?

Williams, P: No, no. They seemed their usual selves the last time I saw them. Nothing out of character. Please, please find them.

DS Mayhew: We're doing our absolute best, but we need your help too, Pastor Williams. Someone will be around the church soon. We'll also need to talk to your wife again.

Williams, P: Yes, of course. Anything we can do to help.

DS Mayhew: Thank you for your time. You are free to go.

Interview terminated at 5:17 p.m.

Police interview transcript: 012

DS Mayhew: Detective Sergeant Mayhew and Detective Johnson interviewing.

Please state your full name and occupation.

Williams, G: My name is Gifty Nana Efia Kortey-Williams. I am a prophetess at the Holy Spirit Redeemer's Church.

Det. Johnson: Thank you. Is it alright to call you Mrs Williams?

Williams, G: Of course, officer.

DS Mayhew: A conversation that you had with Mrs Mutesi has come to light, and we'd like to talk to you about it.

Williams, G: Yes, my husband mentioned it when he came back. Enid had spoken to me several times over the years about wanting to have more children. She's not the only one. Several wives in our church have the same problem. I can sympathise. I'm the mother of five children, big, strong boys, and naturally, some are eager for the same thing.

DS Mayhew: Okay. And?

Williams, G: And, what's my secret? Well, it's not a big thing, but I . . . I use medicinal herbs from Ghana. The churchwomen know. It's not illegal or juju, but not everyone understands. It's a little secret we have among us. I pray vigorously each time I take the leaves, then I lie down with my husband, and now I have five boys, five big men.

DS Mayhew: And did you give any of these herbs to Mrs Mutesi?

Williams, G: Yes, but nothing happened. Not even a miscarriage or ectopic or anything.

I told her she needed more faith.

Det. Johnson: And what did she say to that?

Williams, G: She agreed, naturally. Enid and Emmanuel are very spiritual, so I can't understand why she's not conceived. Lack of faith can be the only answer.

DS Mayhew: Right. And was Mr Mutesi or anybody else aware of this?

Williams, G: I don't know. I obviously didn't discuss it with him, so I don't know. Sorry, but I don't see the use in this questioning. It's been two over weeks and no trace of them, nothing.

DS Mayhew: We're working round the clock, but I'll be honest with you, the Mutesis appear to be the perfect family. No enemies, no debts, no major issues here or abroad. I can assure you, though, Mrs Williams, that we are doing our absolute best.

Williams, G: Thank you.

DS Mayhew: Now, Mrs Williams, let's talk about the last time you spoke to the Mutesi family.

Williams, G: I've already told you.

DS Mayhew: Did Mrs Mutesi speak to you about the devil or evil or anything like that?

Williams, G: Yes—no, not to me. Enid spoke to my husband briefly after their last service. I can lipread.-

Det. Johnson: Oh, I see. You didn't mention this in your statement or during your first interview.

Williams, G: Hmm, well, I didn't want my husband to know. Besides, it's a church. We discuss spiritual things all the time, and she didn't seem anxious, but I was concentrating on her lips. She asked about Satan. My husband gave her some advice, and that was it.

DS Mayhew: Once again, is there anything else you'd like to tell us?

Any conversations or incidents that you, your husband, or anyone else had with the Mutesi family before their disappearance?

Williams, G: No. Nothing at all. That's it. We talked about God and my husband's sermon and Enid's work and how thankful she was for God's providence in her life etc., and then they left.

Det. Johnson: How much do you charge for your herbs, Mrs Williams?

Williams, G: It's not illegal, officer; it's not weed. I go through customs, and they check and say it's fine. I can give you the list of herbs if you like. Can you read Twi? I could make a lot a lot of money selling these things online, but I only charge a hundred pounds for a big packet. Most of the churchwomen pay me in instalments. I make it very easy for them.

Det. Johnson: And how much did Mrs Mutesi owe you?

Williams, G: Nothing. She would give me twenty-twenty pounds. She finished paying for the last packet months ago.

Det. Johnson: And do you declare tax on this little business of yours, Mrs Williams? Anyway, we have more pressing matters. Do you have proof that Mrs Mutesi paid you the full amount for your herbs?

Williams, G: What? It's not a business! I do it for my sisters in Christ. If I could do it for free, I would, but I get them from Ghana, which costs money. I make no profit, and no, I don't have proof that Enid paid me. Maybe you can check her bank account, I don't know. Will you tell my husband? Am I going to be arrested?

DS Mayhew: No, of course not. Is there anything else that you've forgotten to tell us? We need to know.

Mrs Williams: No, no, no. I'm sorry. I should have mentioned all this before. I don't want my husband to find out. Please. I'm sorry. But I swear to you on this holy book here, that I am not withholding any information from you.

DS Mayhew: Okay, fine. But Mrs Williams, if any other details of your interactions with the Mutesi family come to mind, you must let us know. Thank you for your time; you are free to go.

Interview terminated at 4:07 p.m.

Police interview transcript: 053

DS Mayhew: Detective Sergeant Mayhew and Detective Johnson interviewing.

Please state your full name and occupation.

Ugwe, C: Constance Mary Ugwe. Factory worker.

DS Mayhew: Thank you for coming to see us. Can I call you Mrs Ugwe? We've been trying to track you down for weeks.

Ugwe, C: Sorry, I'm so, so sorry. My solicitor said you promise not to give me problems if I talk to you.

Det. Johnson: Yes, that's right. We've promised to overlook any immigration issues with anyone connected to the Mutesi case. Please could you tell us about your relationship with Emmanuel and Enid Mutesi?

Ugwe, C: It's not that I don't want to help, *mngu nirehemu*. We're close. I used to collect Rachel from school when Emmanuel was too busy. We call each other all the time.

Det. Johnson: What did you talk about?

Ugwe, C: Everything. The church. Family. How hard it is in this country.

Det. Johnson: Did the Mutesis ever speak to you about any specific problems they had? Any worries or concerns?

Ugwe, C: Life isn't easy, sir. Whenever I'm missing my children, Enid would come to my place and pray and cry with me. They've been very good to me here on my own. I'm a widow.

DS Mayhew: Were you aware of any problems that the family was having?

Ugwe, C: We all have personal problems.

DS Mayhew: I appreciate that, but we need to know anything specific that can help us with our investigation. Mrs Ugwe. Mrs Ugwe, I'm waiting.

Ugwe, C: It's a lot of rubbish, but someone told me once that they saw Emmanuel coming out of a betting shop. It's not true. Emmanuel is a good man.

DS Mayhew: Could you provide us with the name of the person, please? Mrs Ugwe, I asked you a question. Mrs Ugwe, you need to provide us with the name of the person now; otherwise, you will be obstructing an active police investigation.

Ugwe, C: Eunice. Eunice Kabaka. We fellowship with her. She's a liar.

DS Mayhew: And did you speak to either Enid or Emmanuel about the allegations made by Eunice Kabaka?

Ugwe, C: No. I asked Enid how she was doing, and she said fine, but—

DS Mayhew: What?

Ugwe, C: No, nothing. I've forgotten. She said they were all fine.

DS Mayhew: Mrs Ugwe, please try to remember everything that Mrs Mutesi told you.

It could help us.

Ugwe, C: I've forgotten, I can't remember.

Det. Johnson: Did you know about the fertility issues that the Mutesis were having?

Mrs Ugwe?

Ugwe, C: It's private.

DS Mayhew: Mrs Ugwe, what have I just said? We need your help to find your friends.

Any withholding of information could impede our investigation.

Ugwe, C: I know.

DS Mayhew: So, I'll ask you again, do you know anything about Emmanuel and Enid Mutesi's fertility issues?

Ugwe, C: Pastor Williams's wife was helping them.

DS Mayhew: And did Eunice speak to you about this?

Ugwe, C: Yes. She wasn't happy. Please, please don't tell Pastor Williams. Please, I beg you.

His wife told the women to keep her herbs a secret, or God would punish them, close their wombs forever. But, the herbs, don't work. They were making Eunice sick, and she was struggling to pay for them. Mrs Williams told her that she was bad and lacked faith. She told her that if she bought them and prayed more, she'd have another baby.

DS Mayhew: Do you know if Mr Mutesi was aware of this situation?

Ugwe, C: *Mngu, sijui.* I don't know! Enid told me a few months ago that they were struggling. I even gave her some money. But then it passed.

Det. Johnson: Can you explain further?

Ugwe, C: I don't know, I don't know. Things got better. Enid was feeling down and then she was fine.

Det. Johnson: And that was it? Mrs Ugwe?

Ugwe, C: Uh? Yes, I mean, sorry.

Det. Johnson: What are you thinking about?

Ugwe, C: Nothing. Only the last Sunday I saw them in church. I was going to skip service. I was tired. I clean people's houses, it's too hard that job. But Enid begged me to come.

Det. Johnson: Why?

Ugwe, C: She wanted me to meet somebody.

DS Mayhew: Who?

Ugwe, C: Some people, *wazungu*, white people. From America.

DS Mayhew: What? Did you meet them?

Ugwe, C: Yes. I didn't see them during service, but they were there afterwards, in the car park. They were nice.

DS Mayhew: You spoke to them?

Ugwe, C: Yes, but not for long.

DS Mayhew: Mrs Ugwe, this is extremely important. Can you give us a description of these people? Do you have names, addresses? You need to provide us with as much information as you can.

Ugwe, C: Why, sir? We get visitors to the church all the time. Guest speakers from all over the world, the Philippines, South America, different, different African countries.

They're not the first Americans to come and visit us.

DS Mayhew: How did Mrs Mutesi know these people? These visitors?

Ugwe, C: I don't know, she didn't tell me. She just wanted me to meet them. What were their names? Something like Martin and something, I've forgotten.

DS Mayhew: A description. Can you provide us with a full description of their appearance?

Ugwe, C: Yes. They were white. The lady had very dark curly hair, like a weave-on. The man had dark yellow hair.

DS Mayhew: Anything else? It really is vital that you give us as much information as you can about them.

Ugwe, C: Why? They're church people. Smiling, laughing, happy to be with us.

DS Mayhew: I know it's been a few weeks, but you must provide us with as much detail about these people as possible so that we can locate them and speak to them.

Ugwe, C: Okay, okay. The man was tall, skinny. He had a shirt and pants, light-coloured pants, I think. The woman, she had curly hair, very thick. She was skinny and wearing a shirt and long skirt, I think.

DS Mayhew: And you spoke to them?

Ugwe, C: Yes. Briefly. They said they were happy to be in the UK. Enid seemed to be a bit excited. I don't know why. Then they left, and Eunice and Emmanuel left, and that was it.

DS Mayhew: Thank you for this information, Mrs Ugwe. Ryan, did you get that?

Det. Johnson: Yep, all noted.

DS. Mayhew: Good. I want you to put out an APW. Er, let's have a word outside. One moment, Mrs Ugwe.

Ugwe, C: Oh. I hope I've not said anything wrong.

DS. Mayhew: No. We have to look into all lines of inquiry, we won't be long.

Interview paused at 09:09 a.m.

Det. Johnson: Detective Johnson and Detective Sergeant Mayhew with Mrs Constance Ugwe.

DS. Mayhew: Mrs Ugwe, we're bringing in somebody for questioning, so we'd like you to stay here whilst we're conducting the interview, and then we'll be back to wrap things up. Is that okay? Would you like a tea, coffee, a cold drink?

Ugwe, C: No, thank you. How long will I have to be here for? I'm late for work.

DS. Mayhew: I promise we won't be much longer. I'll get you some water.

If you need anything, please knock on the door, and my colleague will come.

Ugwe, C: What? Have I been arrested? I haven't done anything wrong. I don't know where Enid and Emmanuel are. I've told you everything I know.

DS. Mayhew: Mrs Ugwe, you are helping us with our inquiries, but we need you to hang on a little longer. We have to go now, but please bear with us.

Interview paused again at 10:49 a.m.

Police interview transcript: 054

DS Mayhew: Detective Sergeant Mayhew and Detective Inspector Carlisle interviewing. Please state your full name and occupation.

Williams, P: Pastor Paul Williams, Holy Spirit Redeemer's Church.

DS. Mayhew: We have brought you into the station to be interviewed under caution as some new information has come to light. You do not have to say anything, but anything you do say may be given as evidence in a court of law. You have the right to stop this interview at any time and seek legal representation. Do you understand, Pastor Williams?

Williams, P: Yes, but what is all this? I have nothing to hide. Have you found them?

DS. Mayhew: You previously provided us with a list of all attendees at the Holy Spirit Redeemer's Church service of Sunday the seventeenth of March, is that correct?

Williams, P: Yes, that's correct.

DS. Mayhew: I am presenting Pastor Williams with the list of attendees he provided to police. Please can you confirm that this is the final and definitive list of attendees at the church service?

Williams, P: Yes. Yes, the list is correct. Why?

DS. Mayhew: We have reason to believe that there were two other attendees at the church service on the seventeenth of March who are not on this list. We have previously discussed with you why CCTV footage of the car park from the day of the Mutesi's disappearance was recorded over. You said that this is standard practice. However, we now have reason to believe that this may have been done to hide the presence of some visitors to the church.

Williams, P: Nonsense! You have interviewed the members who were at the service, and they've all told you the same thing. I've already told you that we don't have the means or the space to save CCTV footage; that's why we scrub it regularly. It's the truth.

D.I Carlisle: And who would normally scrub and reset the CCTV footage, Mr Williams?

Williams, P: Sometimes it's myself, sometimes Emmanuel, but I think on that occasion, I did it because I had the time, nothing unusual in that. There were no extra attendees.

DS. Mayhew: What about a couple from America? Do you remember two such people attending the service, perhaps towards the end? Pastor Williams?

Williams, P: But, but it was nothing. Who told you? They were just two tourists who came to say hello and then left. They came for five minutes and left.

D.S Mayhew: Pastor Williams, can I remind you that you are under caution, and anything you say or do may be given as evidence in a court of law. That means that if you lie to us, you could be charged with lying under caution, which carries a custodial sentence if found guilty.

Williams, P: How dare you threaten me! I am a man of God, and may the Lord strike me dead if I am lying to you.

D.I Carlisle: We've carried out some further checks into your finances. I am now presenting Pastor Williams with a photocopy of a bank passbook. The account holder is a Mr Ezekiel Kwesi Williams, your son. On the eighth and fifteenth of March, money was deposited into this account, totalling some forty thousand US dollars. We've made further inquiries, and this money was wired from Galveston, Texas. Would you care to explain?

Williams, P: Eze's finances are none of my business.

DS. Mayhew: How old is your son, Pastor Williams?

Williams, P: He's seventeen.

D.I Carlisle: How does a seventeen-year-old kid get access to that amount of money?

You better start telling us the truth, or it won't only be God you'll be up against. Two days after the final transaction was made into your son's account, an American couple appeared at your church. However, not one church member remembers seeing them. Funny that. A few hours later, the Mutesi family went missing. We need a truthful explanation right now.

Williams, P: I want my solicitor.

D.I Carlisle: Fine. Interview terminated at 18:04 p.m.

The Tottenham and Wood Green Independent: Bodies, Possibly of Tottenham Family, Found in Hertfordshire.
Friday, 4 July 2019

On 3rd July 2019, a car containing three bodies was recovered from a secluded area of Bowyer's Water, Hertfordshire, after a tip-off from a member of the public.

Formal identification is underway, but it has been confirmed that the car registration matches that of Emmanuel Mutesi, a Ugandan man living in Tottenham, who has been reported missing along with his wife and child since March.

Two people, aged forty-three and fifty-one, have been arrested in connection with the disappearance of the Mutesi family. They are thought to be a local church pastor and his wife, both of whom were known to the Mutesi family.

An international arrest warrant has also been issued for an American couple in connection with the family's disappearance. They are described as Caucasian, possibly from Texas, and between the ages of thirty-five and fifty. An e-fit of the couple can be found on the Crimestoppers website.

Friends of the family, who spoke to the TWG Independent on condition of anonymity, have accused the Mutesi's local church, the Holy Spirit Redeemer, of being involved in the family's disappearance. One person known to the family said, 'We want answers. People are saying that the church arranged for some people to help the family with something, but it went wrong and now they're gone. There's even talk of organ trafficking, and I don't know what else. How can something like this happen in this country?'

Anyone who has information in connection with this case should call the police or visit the Crimestoppers website.

NYABINGI IS AWAKE
Alain Patrick IRERE HIRWA

Part I: They Mess Up In Their Own Country

Around 1917, three Belgian minor seminary students were sent to spread the word of the Lord in Rwanda. Claude, François, and Yves were infamous. They liked doing a litany of not-so-holy things, including jerking off in the school bathroom on Sundays. On one such Sunday, just after the evening prayers, as usual, Claude went into the bathroom first, clutching a black and white magazine of naked girls. His partners in crime stayed outside, looking out for him, just in case. François went in second. He had just disappeared into a stall when Justus, the old Priest, came out of his office to conduct his regular inspection. In Justus's book, cleanliness was equal to godliness, and toilets were no exception. Claude and Yves intercepted him at the stall door François had just entered. They spoke quickly to divert his attention, then led him deftly to the next door. Justus dutifully completed his inspection of the bathrooms and, by the look on his face, was satisfied that a mass could be held in them. Once Justus was out of sight, François emerged, still zipping his pants. Yves gave him a high five before going in to take his turn.

There is a game children play called hide and seek. I sucked at it as a child. In my folly, I would cover my eyes and assume that if I couldn't see the seeker, they couldn't see me either. François and his partners were guilty of similar foolishness. Justus was far more cunning than his holy garb suggested. He played along with their ruse, then returned to spy on them through the window. His suspicions confirmed, he burst into the bathroom and caught Yves with his pants down, literally.

Since this story is titled 'Nyabingi is Awake', you are probably guessing it has something to do with Africa. Well observed, the dark continent is indeed its setting. See, as punishment, Justus decided to send the boys to this newly discovered territory to spread the word of the Lord as missionaries. The details of their crossing, the parts where they board the ship and sail across the ocean, are boring, filled with seasickness and saltwater spray, so I'll skip it. They ended up in Rwanda; that's what matters.

Part II: They Arrive In Rwanda

Like all good missionaries, François, Claude, and Yves set off into the unknown. They fought their way through inhospitable wastelands and dense jungles. They grew beards and developed dark tans. Gahima, a skinny 15-year-old Rwandan boy, guided them. Along the way, Gahima killed two snakes that were about to bite the bazungu and single-handedly fought a hyena that wanted a taste of this new white flesh.

I am trying to get you to believe that they relied on the strength and wit of a mere 15-year-old to reach their destination, which is to say, none of this actually happened. I can lie to you; it is my story. I do what I want with it.

Gahima led them to the king's palace, where the old monarch had organised a party for his new white friends. That party was fire. Today's event organisers promise that their parties will be lit.

You get there, and you can't even find someone who can light your cigarette. But, of course, this is irrelevant to the story, or is it?

The king's party was literally lit. Truly lit. Since they did not have electricity back then, there was wood fire everywhere. Half-naked girls danced igishakamba, and young men sipped banana wine and bragged about how many enemies they had castrated on the battlefield. As was the practice in those days, the men showed off enemy testicles to attract girls—all in a bid to dip their own testicles in them. If I was a great soldier back then, I would have opened up a shop for dead enemies' testicles where less great men would come and buy some and go home and lie to their wives about their achievements.

The next day, the king gave the missionaries a tour. They encountered the purest forms of melanin and a barrage of uncivilised rituals. As they toured, they paused now and again to bestow blessings on naked little black kids playing urukiramende. Jean had never seen a kid jump that high; it reinforced his belief in evolution. He was sure that if these kids trained hard enough, they could even climb up trees like monkeys.

Further along, they encountered a family who had arrived with a bunch of cows to offer to the king. François asked the king if he had ordered them to bring the cattle; the king was like, 'Nah, I don't even know those dudes! But it's cool, isn't it?' or something like that.

As they were touring the rural villages, the king spotted a young woman clad in her inshabure. He almost fainted. That babe was an angel. Being the king, he beckoned her over, and she came with a dazzling catwalk swing, shaking her ass up the social ladder. She had all the qualities that the king was into: ass, long neck, black gum, and fabulous amasunzu. He already had a few wives, but all cows and women belonged to him. He could do with them whatever he pleased, just as I can do with this story that is mine. I can delete everything right now and start writing in Kinyarwanda.

Talking about Kinyarwanda, this story would have been a hundred times better in Kinyarwanda. I see languages the same way I see my wife and side chicks. Kinyarwanda is the wife who took my virginity when I was young, the wife who stands by me through thick and thin, the wife my parents loved when they first met her. Then there is French, the first side chick, a colonial language. The thing about side chicks is they always look way hotter than the wife but aren't really. They are temporary, yet they can leave behind a wave of chaos. One of the main rules of hoe-nation is that as soon as a side chick starts to behave like the main chick, replace her with a new side chick: something Rwanda understands. So French was quickly replaced by English, my second-hand colonial language, even though Rwanda was never colonised by England. And like a man with a wife and too many side chicks, I became somewhat confused. I used to think in Kinyarwanda, but because of our colonial school system, I started to think in French. And now, I struggle to think in English even as I tell this story. Of course, this is irrelevant to the story, or is it?

Where were we? Ah yes, the young woman. After carefully checking her out, the king took her home, leaving her man standing in the woods, rejoicing that his woman was beautiful enough to be chosen by royalty. I know. I don't get it too, but trust me, I am not making this up. That is how it was.

On their way back, Yves mentioned something about needing some land to build a church on, and the king gave him a piece of stick.

King: Take this stick; throw it as far as you can. Wherever it lands, that's your land. Build, eeh, what is it that you want to build again?'

The moral of this story is generosity: the king takes home

somebody else's wife, no big deal; the king gives a white guest a piece of land, no big deal. Or is it?

Yves: A church.

King: What is a church?

Yves: You see, you and your people have lived in sin since you were born, and we want to build a house where you can come and get purified. That is a church. If you don't come to our church, bad things will happen. But you don't need to worry. There is this guy called Jesus; he is a really cool dude. He can walk on water. Can you believe that?'

The king laughed out loud as he turned to his umwiru; they both laughed in unison.

King: We did that. We went to conquer Ikinyaga by boat. We were walking on water, right?

Yves: No, this man walked on water with his feet. No boat.

King: No way!

Yves: Yes! This man, Jesus, was sent by God to save all of us sinners. If you guys don't come along, Burundi is going to conquer your territory. The crops will dry; no rain will fall on your land. Your people will hate you.

King: Get outta here. We have abavubyi. They call rain when we need it. It's all good.

Yves: Don't say I didn't warn you, but let's build it and see how it goes.

Yves handed the king his bottle of whiskey. The king took a sip, and it was good. He turned to his umwiru with a serious face.

King: Convene all abiru. I need to wed this new bride as soon as possible.

The umwiru nodded.

Rwandans have always been double-tongued. It is in our blood. Later that night, the king with his trusted abiru would sit together, not to talk about the new bride but to decide how to rid themselves of the white people who, according to news from Kongo, had decimated entire villages. Gathered in one of the thatched huts, which served as the king's palace, were the country's most righteous and wisest elders. It was their job to advise the king on how to deal with everyday threats. The king's spear was thrust in front of his own hut, a 'Do Not Disturb' sign. He was still having a private moment with his new bride, who was not keeping it private at all. The moans could be heard outside, but no one really paid attention. It was around the time Rwandans discovered the art of squirting, and women were having the time of their lives. The whole country was like one big BangBros outdoors set.

Squirting, why have we not yet patented this art? It is our discovery, and no one knows. Shame. Next time you squirt, or make her squirt, scream Rwanda out loud.

They all stood up when the king finally emerged. He had to bend over to enter the hut's low entrance, which also happened to be an exit. Their architects must have had a real sense of humour—who in their right mind built entrances and exits that low for such tall people?

The king took a seat on his throne made of leopard skin. His new bride handed him his smoking pipe before joining other women in the backyard, where they were preparing food and drinks. He listened as they plotted, devising military strategies to combat the white people.

King: They have some real dope alcohol, though. I liked it.

Silence fell as they all put their banana wine-filled jugs down.

The thing about power is that even when you are wrong, you are treated as right.

King: My trusted friends, this is no ordinary enemy. These fuckers killed our neighbours' kings when they tried to fight them. They were our enemies, but they didn't deserve to be disgraced like that.

Umwiru: Have you heard of their weapons that spit fire?

King: Yeah, guns. I saw them today. They never put them down.

Umwiru: What do they want?

King: They say they want a land to build a house for their god, but we all know they have other plans. Maybe tomorrow, they will ask me to pray to their god. Maybe they will take our youth away as they did in Kongo.

Umwiru: I say we kill them. I need some white testicles to add to my collection.

They all laughed aloud.

King: We lost most of our best fighters in the Karagwe war. We are shorthanded at the moment. They killed dozens in the Kongo. Everywhere they go, they wipe out everything in their way. We need better than our spears to fight them.

Umwiru: You mean we need guns?

King: Yeah, but most importantly, we need to be smart. When they ask for the land to build their house, give them the Nyabingi hill. Let's see how their god likes it there.

Umwiru: I don't know how to shoot the guns. My King, can you shoot a gun?

King: You don't know how to shoot anything, Kagina. Just stick to the thinking and fucking. That is all we need you for.

They all laughed and continued drinking.

The next day, the missionaries started recruiting young men to build their church. After the first workday, they gave them tiny objects called coins that supposedly had great value. That is how I have ended up here, staying up this late, working for money when I should have been chilling somewhere in the forest with my cows or having my testicles chopped off. Bastards.

PART III: They mess up in Rwanda

Bwiza, a 14-year-old girl who lived with her mother, was sweeping the veranda when a soldier rushed inside the compound. Her mother was inside the hut worshipping Ryangombe. Bwiza called her mother since girls were not allowed to talk to strangers. The soldier delivered the news that her husband and son had died in the war against Karagwe.

Bwiza's mother cried for three days, nonstop. Seriously. That was how deep her love was. When she stopped crying, Bwiza told her about these white people recruiting young girls and boys to work in their church. Bwiza's mother slapped her twice to check if she was out of her mind.

Bwiza's mother: You want to worship another god? Our god answers us through Ryangombe, here in our home. Who needs to walk to find God? God finds us.

Bwiza: Did your god answer your prayers? They are dead, aren't they?

Bwiza's mother started crying again until she fell asleep. Bwiza packed her bags. Did they have bags? Leather bags? I am not sure. The point is that she disobeyed her mother and went to serve the bazungu's god.

Bwiza was well received by these holy priests (François, Yves, Claude), who introduced her to Jesus, the Holy Spirit, and the Father-God. They told her how these three gods made one god; it didn't make sense to her at first, but they assured her that she would figure it out with time.

Those priests were generous. They gave Bwiza a marvellous small object called a mirror. Bwiza used it to look at her face and, for the first time, witnessed its beauty with absolute clarity. They also gave her a matchbox containing sticks she could use to make a fire in the blink of an eye, without having to rub stones against each other for what seemed like an eternity. They taught her how to read letters they had brought from their country. They taught her mathematics, the art of counting complicated things, sometimes intangible like X and Y. They were so cool.

One day, Bwiza was cleaning the church. Claude was seated in one of the pews, praying. His eyes were half-closed. They hadn't given Bwiza clothes yet, so she still wore her inshabure, which meant she was topless. As she bent over to put candles on the altar, her breasts swung in Claude's direction. He opened his eyes, and they met hers. She shyly offered a thin smile. That was a turn-on. Claude stood up and approached Bwiza with a taut look on his face, trying to convey his position of power.

He touched her face and then caressed her arms, thinking of a smooth French pick-up line. Something like, 'Let's flip a coin. Heads, you're mine; tails, I'm yours.' But he didn't feel like asking. Why ask for something when you can take it? he thought. Besides, having a go at this girl was no big deal if it brought him little joy as he continued the difficult work of bringing civilisation to Rwanda. His joy, however short-lived, was the price to be paid for the great work he was doing in Rwanda. Bwiza was just collateral damage. So he moved his hands slowly up Bwiza's neck. She tolerated his impunity until she remembered her mother's words: 'No man should ever touch you, ever! Not even your husband.' Immediately, she pulled herself free and fled. Claude didn't bother chasing after her; he had his partners in crime. He headed outside and found his pals smoking cigarettes. They conspired and approached the church when Bwiza was inside. Yves quietly closed all the doors, and they encircled the poor girl who found herself trapped. She tried to run, but they had all the exits covered. Yves caught her by her hair and dragged her to the altar, where they bound her arms and had her legs wide open.

Claude quickly unzipped his pant and moved it down to his knees; the other two stood by looking out for him, just in case. Bwiza cried out in pain, struggling to push Claude's heavy body off her in vain. Claude put his hand on her mouth to keep her quiet;

she bit it and spat his blood back in his face. This didn't stop him; if anything, it egged him on. He kept thrusting, trying to penetrate her. She yelled as loudly as she could, hoping that one of her friends would hear her and come to her rescue. Bwiza's cries fell on deaf ears; her friends were having a choir rehearsal outside, raising their voices as they tried the Western method, solfege. They were on a tight schedule. They had been told by the missionaries that they had to impress a special guest, a priest who was journeying from Kongo to celebrate the Easter mass.

I love to research. I research everything. An apartment I want to move into, a girl I like, a beer I want to try out. Everything.

But Claude and his partners in crime were not like me. They hadn't done any research about the land the king gave them. Nyabingi's tomb happened to be in the middle of that church, underneath the altar.

Bwiza's cry was so loud it echoed through the earth and reached the spirits in the underworld. Contrary to Christianity's beliefs, the underworld is an eternal resting place for heroes, a peaceful reward for all the good deeds done while still alive. Of all the thousands of hills in Rwanda, Nyabingi asked her followers to bury her on this specific hill. Like Sheldon, she had many reasons to claim it as her spot. Standing at the top of this hill, one could see both the Muhabura volcano and the Akanyaru river. Fire and Water. War and Peace.

The air outside the church suddenly became windy and cold. The kind of cold that would make exhaled carbon dioxide visible when one spoke. The kind of cold that would have been noticed by any sane person, given how sudden it came to be. Out of the winds came distinguishable figures, spirits that looked like human-shaped clouds, intertwined in couples. Even in the afterlife, spirits were assigned partners except those who died virgins. As Bwiza's cry grew louder, one specific spirit, feminine and fiery, opened its eyes and made for the church. Nyabingi had died a virgin after turning down countless great men, including kings. Although beautiful with very feminine features, she was a deadly warrior. She had set one condition for any man who wished to bed her: he would have to defeat her in a fight. No man was able to defeat her in her lifetime.

Back at the altar, Bwiza's eyes were closed to the pain Claude's onslaught inflicted on her. Her sobs echoed through the church. Out of nowhere, another woman's voice rose, filling the whole church with beautiful, sad harmony. It rose and rose before changing tone, turning suddenly to anger. A chorus of spells and incantations echoed through the church. Claude turned and noticed a human-shaped cloud gliding toward him. He thought he was hallucinating and reached for the wine glass on the altar. As he took a sip, he saw a figure staring at him from the reflection on the glass. He dropped the vessel, hands trembling. The image he saw was a dense white cloud with dark shades that formed a woman's facial features. It looked like a horror monochrome painting, but this painting was emitting red fumes that yelled angry incantations.

François, who watched the spectacle unfold, suddenly leapt into action. Using all his strength, he pulled Claude off Bwiza. The spirit was unmoved. Or rather, it did move but through him, disappearing for a moment. He felt a sudden pain in his chest and fell like a tree trunk that had been cut through. His forehead landed on a sharp stair, and his body followed. The spirit watched them with eyes that looked like hell. I honestly don't know what hell looks like, but her eyes were fiery red. Yves and Claude ran towards the door. Behind them, Bwiza started to roar a raspy incantation that perfectly matched the spirit's crescendo. She was no longer powerless. She stood up slowly and said, 'Where do you guys think you're going? I haven't cum yet!'

The hunt began.

ELEGY OF AN ERNE
Alex Kadiri

Eyes, all have them, but some more than others.

In all her adult years, Kamsi has never spent a Christmas in Lagos. The Igbos never do this, at least not the ones who know their left from their right or who know not to leave out the *g* in Igbo. Lagos is where she works as a struggling nurse in a small, understaffed private hospital in Ojuelegba. It is where she lives in a tenement—not too far from work—that smells like *ogiri* and poverty, where she hopes a man with a secure job will one day marry and liberate her from the pressures of unmarried life. To Kamsi, Lagos is for toiling, for sweating, and her village in Oraifite is for unwinding. When you've spent eleven months doing backbreaking work in a foreign land, it is only fitting that you take a month off to straighten that back and splurge your pennies someplace where envious eyes can see.

For years now, it has been like this—scrounge in Lagos, swagger in the village. Her mother did not sell rice from a wheelbarrow to raise a nonstarter. First week of every December, she empties her bank account, divides the money in two and takes one half to Aswani where clothes are cheaper than bubble gum and where if you're weak-willed, traders will buy the pants off your buttocks. The other half is for Oraifite and the keen village eyes that will gauge her success that year. This half she expends putting up appearances—like the flight ticket she buys so that her luggage can carry those white airport tags that sit on the handle and announce you did not come by road, or the remainder that she squanders on crates of Amstel Malta and goat meat peppersoup, so her relatives can sweat and mouth-breathe and wash down the spiciness to the admiration of neighbours.

But this year is not like others. Like before, Oraifite will still see her, but this December, her mission is different. There is a question that troubles her mind so implacably she is going home to seek answers. Surely, her mother must have them. She has answers to everything: who is destined for hell, whose Christmas rice to discard because it's been laced with poison. She entertains superstitions too: trees where witches converge, rivers that swallow strangers, shape-shifting cats. And so, there is none better equipped for Kamsi's questions than her.

Another thing that is different this year is Kamsi's mode of transport. She has opted for road travel because the year has been especially unkind. She might have to lie about bad weather or say the tag came off somehow.

Right now, she is in a room too small for a claustrophobe, stuffing the last of her things into a brown holdall with tired seams and an embarrassing ink smudge. She looks around with urgency, pauses, and grabs a bottle of lotion; into the bag it goes. She hunkers down, snatches a pair of floral-patterned flip-flops purchased on account of this trip; in it goes. Again she pauses, glances at the gold-rimmed wall clock and wipes her face with the dirty camisole from yesterday. The camisole moistens from her sweat, and she sends it flying. Now she pulls out a wad of cash, counts hastily and hisses. If only she hadn't suffered all that guilt and then gotten distracted at work until she was fined for tardiness. There was also that accursed surge in rent. She hisses again. She'd have to make do. She flips open her compact and stares in its round mirror; her lips are still a perfect red, unmarred by the camisole. She clamps them twice, flips and sends the makeup into the bag. One last time, she checks to see that she hasn't forgotten anything. Satisfied, she zips and lifts the bag with a grunt. It is almost five.

Written, it effaces; etched in stone, it abides.

Daylight is still weak from last night's sleep when Japhet Nsofor arrives at the bus park from the bungaloid suburbs where he lives. He is a small man with a shaved head, lugging a plastic suitcase and sweating even though the sun hasn't clocked in. A danfo ride from Badagry to Volks will do that to you. The vehicles are rickety and meander through roads that look war-torn. Add to that the airlessness and the crammed benches that leave no legroom, and voila, you have an oven. In his right hand is a white handkerchief. He dabs his forehead as he approaches the assigned Hiace. His suitcase follows behind, vibrating on the tarmac. There is a queue. The passengers are already filing in, most of them speaking Igbo. Behind the minibus, two men are working out the economics of bags and suitcases and cramming them into the meagre luggage space. He checks the number on his ticket and wonders if Seat 13 will be conducive. Then he joins the back of the queue. He is the last one.

A minute passes before someone taps his shoulder.

'You wan carry am for leg?'

He hands over the suitcase and watches as the man rolls it. He inhales, notices how the air is still pregnant with dew and how his sweat is already drying. He checks his bladder—neither full nor empty. Regardless, he should find the urinal. It will stink, but better that than lengthening their trip with pee breaks. He checks his wristwatch—two minutes to spare before the bus leaves at six. Because it's his first time using this park, he taps the woman in front. They are of the same height, but for a woman, she is average, not short.

'Please, where is the toilet?'

The woman turns to him, and there is a fleeting moment in which he thinks she shudders. She does not respond; she just stares, as though stunned, as though a poltergeist has just materialised. The colour drains from her face; her lips start to quiver. But his appearance isn't grisly, so he wonders what this is about. He repeats the question. She stays mute, appears even to be avoiding his gaze like people do the sun. But then her eyes lock with his as though she cannot help it, as though there is something in his that beguiles. Perhaps there is something on his face, he thinks, or on his ears. He checks his ears for soapsuds. Finding none, his forehead creases, his body tenses. What is this woman's deal? He feels himself becoming agitated and adjusts his weight onto his left foot. Then he thumbs the puckered scar above his right cheek. Maybe that is it.

But it surely isn't because, the next instant, the woman is on the ground, breathless and incoherent as she struggles to speak. Her legs are splayed in front of her. Like ash run through by gale, the queue disperses. Hasty feet tread the tarmac. Heads peek out from the bus. Travellers mill about as though they have all the time in the world. A man dashes over, a woman too. Hands go under her armpits and around her back to keep her upright. Finally, her senses return, and the babbling becomes lucid.

'I need to tell you something,' she whispers through red lips. Her voice is wrapped with distress, her eyes aimed at Japhet.

Kamsi feels like a fraud as she watches this stranger's alarm. The collapse was contrived. But Nigerians, being Nigerians, do not believe anything unless it is garnished with drama. Besides, you do not tell someone 'I just saw you die' in the same way you say 'nice shirt', not unless you're aiming for disbelief. The other travellers stare. It is not her first premonition, but it is the first one she will voice. Too many people have died from her silence, which feels no different to complicity. But until now, she couldn't help it. She has always dreaded the outcome: tell the wrong stranger they will die, and the next minute, you're wearing a car tyre around your neck, fending off blows, and gasping gasoline because you're a *ritualist*. She fears being wrong too. But more than that, she is terrified of being right. Where being wrong makes her a liar, being right makes her something much worse, an executioner.

Seeing a person's death before it happens fills you with guilt. It infects you with sorrow and regret at being incapacitated. You know what is to come, but your hands are tied, so you feel like an accessory. She remembers the first time it happened. She was twelve and in junior secondary. It was shortly after her father's death. She'd just left Oraifite to live with Uncle Nedu, her father's younger brother, in Lagos. She'd been at school, sweaty and in a pinafore, when the vision first seized her. It pinned her gaze to a lad on the school's second-floor balcony and flashed gory images of blood and brain matter in her mind. But she'd chalked it up to puerile imagination. Until another boy whizzed past and sent him screaming, flailing, over the parapet. The boy's head had cracked open like a coconut.

The second time was with a Hausa woman on Uncle Nedu's street. She'd greeted the woman and at once seen flashes of her charred and sprawled out grotesquely like a contortionist. But the woman didn't die that day. She died three days later in an explosion caused by adulterated kerosene. That was when Kamsi knew that something was wrong with her. Without disclosing why, she had gone with her aunt to church to pray away the curse. But like cancer, it remained, tormenting her with unsolicited information. She soon learned that the visions did not follow a strict pattern in their manifestation. Sometimes the ill-fated person croaked right away; other times, after a day or even five. But in every instance, they died.

In truth, Kamsi might have continued to ignore it, but this past year has seen a glut in the number of premonitions—eleven since January, four in the three years prior. It has planted questions in her mind, questions that have sprouted into something more perturbing. Now she wonders if star-crossed persons can be saved. She wonders too if the visions are the only reason the deaths happen, if she is responsible, if she is more than just a harbinger of death. Perhaps she is more like the Grim Reaper than a banshee. It is why she is going home this Christmas—not for the festivities, but to ask these pertinent questions. It is why she is going on the final week of December instead of the first.

She is on her feet now, watching the stranger watch her. He appears to weigh her words, to contemplate their veracity. Around them, the crowd has thinned.

'Don't travel,' she'd told him five minutes earlier, and when he asked why, she'd hesitated, sucked a quick draft of air and stuttered, 'Sometimes, sometimes I see things.'

An incredulous look had crept into the stranger's face then, and his nose had turned up suspiciously. 'What did you see?'

'Accident,' she'd said, preferring the word over 'death'.

He'd backpedalled two steps, his face turning grim. The driver had honked nonstop, and miffed, some onlookers had sucked their teeth, muttering 'God forbid' and melting off into the background to rejoin queues.

The engine revs, and the exhaust fumes. Daylight is rejuvenated. The driver hangs his head out of the driver's side window impatiently. He beckons. He curses. Then he hisses and curses some more. The stranger looks from Kamsi to the driver, he turns, and Kamsi watches him march up to the Hiace. Now it is Kamsi who is alarmed. Hasn't he heard anything she said? This is not what she expected of him. Who chooses death over life?

The first slivers of sunlight spill into the bus park. Two teenage hawkers appear, their wares arranged in steel trays balanced atop their heads. A beggar perambulates, one arm shortened to a stump. Again, the driver curses. His eyes burn like acid.

Honk! Honk!

Japhet knows that the woman's words might bear some truth, that he is being irrational. He should turn around and go home; that is what a normal person would do. But his life is far from normal. He would not have to travel every December if it were. Oraifite is the bane of his existence. While others travel for merrymaking, his trips there are anything but festive. They are to preserve his life because he is his father's firstborn, the one fated to carry the curse.

The way his father told it upon his deathbed, Anansi, their impoverished forebear sold trinkets and artefacts pilfered from the shrine of Amadioha, god of thunder and lightning. Later, seeking protection, he erected a shrine at the back of his compound. This shrine he dedicated to Ikenga, god of strength. For its services, Ikenga made one simple demand—greeting and appeasement at the end of every year, in the form of libation, three he-goats, and a white cock. The animals' blood was to be spattered upon its idol, a dreadful bloodied figurine. In addition, this annual ritual required the presence of the one cursed. Death, he said, was the lot of any accursed descendant who failed to meet these terms. And so, every December, Japhet undertakes this journey so that he can stay alive. It is why he prefers whoremongering to marriage; he hopes to kill the cycle.

Japhet slips his handkerchief into his pocket and ignores his racing heart. It should be the strange woman's turn, but because she is several yards behind, unready, he draws a deep breath and plants one foot on the minibus. Inside, the driver honks and hangs his head out the window.

'Madam, *biko* enter motor let's go!' His face is tighter than new braids.

The woman shakes her head.

'Please, come and remove my bag.'

The driver frowns, alights, and almost convulses as he begins to mutter profanities under his breath. Pairs of eyes peer out the windows now, horrified like children forsaken. At once, everything starts to whirl. Japhet grabs a headrest and collapses into his seat. He shuts his eyes to quell the dizziness. Then he exhales the storm stirring in him and thinks, 'what does it mean?' Perhaps she has seen it because that is his fate until he averts it at Oraifite. Or does it mean Ikenga will not accept his offering this year? When he opens his eyes, the lightheadedness has subsided. The bus is half-empty too. Only four men and two women remain. Now he hears chatter.

'Tsk! Is that why they're going down?'

'Which kind bus I enter today?'

Eyes turn to him and then away. Other pairs steal furtive glances. He can feel the heat of their gaze. He coughs spuriously. The chatter resumes.

'Is it everything people dey believe?'

'Nigerians. So they think this vehicle will crash because of one person?'

Someone scoffs.

'Don't mind them, my brother. Me I dey *kampe*.'

'Me too.'

'We will reach Anambra, and nothing go happen.'

'Unless it's not God I'm serving.'

Now Japhet looks out the window and sees the driver angrier than a cyclone. His finger points furiously at the alighted passengers. They almost come to blows as they shout their arguments in each other's faces like a contest. Japhet sighs, checks his wristwatch: 6:25 a.m. It dawns on him now that this journey will not happen. Nigerians suffer from a severe case of superstition, and this woman has fed it. Yet, he has to be at Oraifite before the New Year. Perhaps he should try a different park.

Boys do not accost him at the second and third parks adjacent to Peace Mass Transit. All buses are grounded at the second; the owner has just died. At the third, a lady chewing gum at the reception tells him that all buses to Anambra have departed; he would have to return tomorrow, but he can buy his ticket now or book online. He hands her the money. Peace Mass Transit is his first choice, but he is sure remnants of today's embarrassment will be waiting for him tomorrow. He waits by the roadside, flagging down danfo after danfo. His legs are just starting to ache when one pulls over. Relieved, he sighs and hops on it. His suitcase goes in the back.

He is slipping his housekey into the rusty keyhole when he hears clipped whistling behind him. At once, three policemen jump out like they're playing hide-and-seek. They seize him, pin his hands behind his back, and slap cold metal around his wrists.

Two things weigh on his mind when they reach the police station—his suitcase that sits unattended outside his door and the appeasement at Oraifite. The latter is why he sweats like an ice-cold Pepsi bottle, why his heart beats like it's on steroids. He is on a deadline. He will have to resolve this quickly. He barks louder than a dog now, but the policemen do not tell him anything. And even though he is unsure who to call—Chizoba or Johnson—they do not let him make a phone call either. Yet, when Chizoba shows up that evening, he isn't surprised to see her; neighbours in tenements tattle more than the network news. He is stunned however that she has not come to bail him.

'Admit what you did,' she tells him.

'Admit what?'

'Stop pretending.'

'What do you mean?'

'First, you try to make me do abortion, then I return home and wake up with blood between my legs. What did you put in my Chivita, Japhet?'

'Wh—what is that supposed to mean, Chizoba?'

'It means what it means.'

Three days whiz past as Japhet languishes in an airless cell. His cellmate is a man with scars and bruises whose eyes are colder than death and whose lips are as silent as they are black. Japhet wonders if the man's crime is murder. Because an answer eludes him, he sleeps like a penguin, with one eye open. In the daytime, he cries, curses, and pleads. They need to believe him, he says. He did not do anything. They need to let him out. His father is dying and needs his medicines. The policemen play deaf. Meanwhile, time moves as though something is chasing after it.

When he is released on conditional bail six days later, Japhet has just over thirty hours left. The ritual only takes about fifteen minutes, so he should be fine if he leaves today. He dashes home to wash off the smell of incarceration. Then he goes from door to door asking about his suitcase, his words hurried and whittled to make up for lost time. He finds it with Mrs Desouza, his middle-aged neighbour, who is diabetic and widowed.

'Don't mention,' she says, adjusting her spectacles, 'it's the least I can do.'

Because a road trip is too steep a risk for a man on the brink of death, he makes for the airport. He will have to fly to Asaba and then continue by road to Anambra. Above him, thunder rumbles.

The airport is a beehive. The attendant tells him he's lucky; there is a flight leaving in forty minutes. Although *lucky* isn't what he feels, he doesn't tell her this. She takes his fare, says there is no five-hundred-naira change, and then grins. 'See how I gave you comfortable seat? Let me take this one as thank you.'

Japhet ponders it momentarily. The Nigerian airport is where you find beggars in suits, corporate beggars. He should tell her off, ask if she hasn't given 'comfortable seats' to everyone who went before him, but right now, reaching Oraifite is all that matters. He makes his way to the escalator and feels woozy on the ride up. Then he joins a small queue, goes barefoot through the doorframe metal detector and past other beggars with scanners, and walks to the waiting area. He is still fiddling with his shoelaces when the announcement comes: *All flights to Asaba have been cancelled.* A sarcastic smile plays on his lips; Amadioha is really out to get him.

He hurries back to the counter.

'Why did they cancel flights?'

'Weather, sir. Thunderstorms on your route. Don't worry, we'll issue a refund.'

Japhet does not wait for the refund. Every second spent in Lagos is a step closer to certain death. He hurries to Ojota Motor Park. It is dusty there, and the vehicles look spent and sedated. A telecommunications mast stands guard beside it, taller than men on stilts. On the sand, black nylons and empty *pure water* sachets dance with the wind.

'The last bus to Anambra just left,' they tell him upon inquiry.

His heart sinks. This cannot be ordinary. Surely, there are forces orchestrating these happenstances. This stinks of Amadioha. His face is glum; his thoughts, haywire. He feels empty, like he is skin and bones with no soul, like he is slough. He would drive if he had a car. Perhaps he should walk.

As he leaves, his feet burdened with indecision, a lanky man with caterpillar moustache approaches him.

'Where you dey go oga?'

'Anambra.'

'Ah! Them don go finish. But I fit carry you.'

Japhet eyes him. He can't be serious.

'I get Sienna.'

'How many passengers remain?'

'No worry about that, *oga*. I go carry only you if you do well. I see say you really need to travel. That's why I want to help you.'

Japhet checks his wrist. His watch is missing. No, it is at the police station. He checks his phone instead: 4:35 p.m.

He pays without hesitation. It is five times the cost.

Three hours later, they are driving through Ore. Daylight has begun to fade, and birds are migrating, ushered home by the failing light. Thoughts fight for space in his head. The fight is vicious, visceral. Finally, one triumphs, and he attempts to shut it out. He does not want to think about it. He fails. Today his mind has a mind of its own. He remembers the strange woman, wonders if the delay has changed anything, or if perhaps this Sienna is what will *take* him.

The windows are wound down, and a steady rush of breeze bathes him. He finds it soothing. Soon his eyes start to close. He is just nodding off when an explosion jolts him wide awake. The car vibrates, then swerves and skids and screeches. His heart leaps. His buttocks tighten and sink deeper into the seat. His right hand hunts for the seatbelt. Before he finds it, the car stops.

'Na just tyre,' the driver says. 'No worry, I have spare.'

He breathes at last.

The rest of the journey is without incident. He is just lugging his bag into his father's compound and thinking to himself that the woman was wrong after all when a kid whose head is covered in white patches of ringworm dashes up to him and reports in heavy Igbo, 'The shrine collapsed last night. It was struck by lightning.'

'Something is wrong with me,' Kamsi tells her mother three days after the incident at Peace Mass Transit.

They are in the outhouse kitchen. Her mother empties a mix of corn and cassava flour into a pot of bubbling water. Then she stirs until the mixture thickens; then the stirring becomes pounding.

Her upper arm heaves with every descent. Now she wipes her forehead with the back of her arm and reties her wrapper.

'Why did you say that?'

'I'm seeing things.'

The woman pours warm water into the pot and resumes pounding. The pot steams and hisses.

'What type of things?'

'Visions. I see people's death before—before it happens.'

She pauses and turns to Kamsi, her forehead creased with questions. She turns the knob now until the flame is weak.

'Did you become born again?'

Kamsi shrugs. 'No. Do you have visions like that?'

'Me? With this my *ukwu*? I don't think there's space in my body for any righteous spirit.'

'What of papa?'

She cackles. 'If your father had any special powers, it was in his penis. That's why you have four step-siblings from different women.'

'Mama, I'm serious.'

'Sorry, my dear. Tell me about it.'

'It's random. The problem is I don't know if they're just visions.'

'What do you mean?'

Kamsi points. 'Check. It's burning.'

Her mother sniffs and turns to the pot.

'Sometimes I think they die because I see it happen. Maybe if I didn't see it—'

'You're blaming yourself? Don't do that.'

She kills the flame now and settles an oversized lid atop the pot. It clangs. She grips Kamsi's shoulders gently and holds her gaze.

'My dear, there is a reason for everything. Perhaps you get these visions so that you can save lives.'

'It doesn't feel that way.'

'Maybe you just haven't learned to accept it. Some gifts can seem like a curse until you teach yourself to embrace them. When I first started selling rice at that polytechnic in Oko, some of my customers called me Madam Nyash. I wanted the ground to open and swallow me. But later, I wore my *thing* with pride, and my curse started to feel like a blessing.'

Kamsi purses her lips in exasperation. 'I'm tired of you.'

'Allow me brag and motivate *biko*.'

They laugh, a robust laugh that swells until it fills the kitchen. When it ebbs, Kamsi is unsure if she shares her mother's conviction. But she agrees that perhaps somewhere in her curse is a gift.

It is New Year's Eve, and Japhet's nostrils are too terrified to breathe. His mouth lends support. A faint noise accompanies every exhale. Although he hasn't slept a wink since the tyre explosion at Ore, his eyes are sharper than an eagle's. All day, he surrounded himself with relatives because the extra pair of eyes would thwart any stealth in death's approach.

Now he is alone in what used to be his father's room, with the aged door ajar because danger is a lover of seclusion. One thought plagues his mind: *How will it happen?* Last night, he visited the Catholic Church near Emeka Offor road and then, against the counsel of De Chidiebere and Aunty Callista—'Don't go and remind Amadioha that it has scores to settle with you'—he visited Amadioha's shrine afterwards to plead for leniency.

'Amadioha will spare you in exchange for a limb,' the pitiless medium told him.

He'd returned home because as much as he loved living, he didn't want to do it handicapped. There was also the pain of dismemberment that he knew he could not take.

Now time is moving too quickly. This minute, he is pacing on the cold concrete; the next, he is sitting on the edge of the bed, his face buried in jittery palms. It continues like this as the clock races.

9 p.m.

10 p.m.

Outside, crickets chirp.

00:15 a.m.

1 a.m.

4 a.m.

7 a.m.

Nothing happens.

It's three days into the new year. Japhet isn't listening as he sits with De Chidiebere, his late father's octogenarian cousin, under a jacaranda. He remembers what he did to Chizoba. He thinks about his spare parts business, to which he cannot yet return until his safety is assured. He thinks about the rubble that sits in place of the shrine, about the appeasement that did not happen. He wonders how he is still alive in the new year.

'Amadioha is not what it used to be,' De Chidiebere explains in a voice as hoarse as it is senile. 'These days, people can shit on its head and go scot-free. It's not like before. Nowadays, mad people eat its sacrifice at junctions, and they don't become madder. Poor people too. Amadioha has lost its potency. It has calmed down. You don't need to worry. It is over.'

Oraifite is a small town, so when Kamsi sees the same star-crossed man that afternoon as she returns from buying meat and spices for peppersoup, she is shocked that he is still alive. It's been more than a week since their first meeting. The man approaches but doesn't see her. He is staring at his phone. Something washes over Kamsi. It is embarrassment. Her heels whirl swiftly, and she steps onto the road, attempting to cross. Her manoeuvre is blind, careless. A horn blares. An oncoming Mitsubishi Pajero spots her and swerves into the man, sending him into the roadside gutter like stone from a catapult.

The man is wet and dead and smelling like piss when they retrieve him. Kamsi covers her ears and screams. Her skin crawls with dread. That evening, when she finally stops shivering, she consoles herself on her mother's bed, resolving to try again and again until she learns to put her gift to good use.

Ten months later, De Chidiebere will erect Ikenga's shrine again because, the week before, a girl called and said her name was Chizoba, and she recently had Japhet's son. Because he has invited her for 'important talk', he will add—to the list of things he plans to tell her—that there was misinformation. Yes, Anansi fell from the palm tree on the last day of the year, but no, he did not die until the third day of the new one. Japhet's father died in March and of natural causes, hence the confusion. De Chidiebere will shake his head dolefully and add to the list that Ikenga's deadline is not the year's end. It is January 3rd.

A NDUMBE MEETING

Uvile Memory Samkelisiwe Ximba

Nothing.

Bare, noisy, choking, silent, screaming, black, blaring, all-but-empty nothing.

That's all Ndumbe saw, felt, understood at that moment. Not the dozen or so faces peering down at her. Not Suzie's slightly amused eyes nor Zola's genuine worry pushing her eyebrows into a bunch.

Nothing.

That's all Ndumbe wanted to say when John deVos pushed through the probing mini mob, shoved his handsome I-just-got-back-from-Greece-tanned face inches from hers, and asked, 'How do you feel?'

Nothing.

'What happened?'

Nothing.

'What's wrong ee-ndoo-mbay?'

The words that forced themselves out of her mouth instead surprised even her. She had to push onto her elbows and rub her head where she'd hit it as she fell. She rubbed it hard just to make sure she was back on earth and knew what she was saying. The

169

crescent of people around her melded into blurs. She shut her eyes, holding out one hand for them to make some space.

'Step back a bit, everyone. Let's give her some room,' John instructed.

Footsteps muffled around the thick boardroom carpet as a few of the onlookers returned to their seats. Only Zola and John's faces towered above her now. Suzie's hovered behind, refusing to miss a bit of the spectacle.

'I—' Ndumbe's throat felt hot and spiky. She grunted slightly to clear the scratch and massaged her neck gently with her fingers.

Zola, noticing this, grabbed a bottle of water from the boardroom table. She knelt beside Ndumbe and held the open bottle to her lips. After gulping almost half the water, Ndumbe pulled back to indicate her satisfaction. She smiled her thanks to her only friend in the room before turning to John.

'What is it, ee-ndoo-mbay?' John asked, crouching next to Zola. His smile did not quite spread the concern he intended to his eyes. Instead, Ndumbe recognised the look she had seen him flash to many of his employees. Annoyance. And impatience. A desire to move on from the interruption Ndumbe's 'episode' had caused.

Pushing up from her elbows so she was at eye level with John and Zola and, with a certainty she did not know she possessed, Ndumbe declared, 'I quit.'

Zola scampered. Three of her stout-legged steps made up one of Ndumbe's, who was powering down the corridor. They were carrying a box each, filled with books, files, and titbits tossed in from the taller woman's desk. In her other hand, Ndumbe clasped her baby bonsai, a gift from her now ex-boyfriend. Everyone was busy in their offices, so the brightly-lit corridors were empty, echoing Ndumbe's hurried departure. Her determined march only faltered and paused when they turned the last corner and stood facing the chunky wooden front doors. Unlike the electricity-illuminated inside, the large glass panels in the front doors let in great pools of light and a glimpse into the world outside their office. A light wind blew spring blossoms into the door, each one knocking tentatively against the glass like little pink flower fairies trying to breathe life into the bland office interior.

Ndumbe sighed gently and watched the blossoms pour, waiting for Zola to finally catch up with her. She turned to look at her friend's cute, concerned face. Her ears were flushed a slight red from her efforts. They just stood there watching one another awhile, Zola catching her breath.

'What am I doing, Zola? What have I done?'

Zola shook her head slowly from side to side and opened and closed her mouth nervously. 'I think you should just go home and rest. You've been through a lot. You know, with the breakup and you getting sick. Maybe you need time.' She tried to assure her friend, who looked dishevelled. 'Plus, it's Friday. You can just take the weekend and call John on Monday. Tell him you hit your head when you fell, and you were just confused, that you love your job.'

Ndumbe nodded at the plan, 'I do love my job.'

Zola continued, 'Yes. Yes, you do. I mean, you're basically all about this job.'

'Yes. Yes, I am. I am.'

They nodded at each other and at their plan. Zola placed her free hand on Ndumbe's arm. 'Everything will be alright.'

'Yes, it will.'

Yet, as they pushed into the blossom rain, she wasn't sure it would be. But she did know that she would not be returning to see those flowers fall there again. That she wouldn't be calling John. When Zola said she'd see her next week, Ndumbe simply muttered, 'Bye, mngani.'

Ndumbe was relieved when she climbed into the Uber, and her driver only grumbled in response to her 'Sanibonani'. Usually, the sour greeting would have irritated her and earned him a one-star at the end of the trip. Today, she settled gratefully into the backseat, quietly eyeing her boxes. After he'd offered to play some music and she'd declined, they simply sat in silence, interrupted only by the tremble of the car and the snatches of life butting in through his open window.

Her phone pinged desperately in her pocket, and she pulled it out. Nosy notifications from her colleagues. Messages selling her car insurance. All the emails she was supposed to attend to after their morning meeting. She pushed the sidebar down, and the phone beeped. 'Ringer off.'

They turned onto the main road that led to Ndumbe's house, gliding past the park she always said she'd take a walk through but never did. The park was the reason she'd moved there two years ago. She'd wanted to come home from work and take long walks in nature. That hopeful, romantic Ndumbe had hoped to have picnics every Sunday with her boyfriend, bathing in the sun or nestled beneath the shadow of the tall trees. Instead, here she was, unemployed, recently broken up, and, as of this morning, a public fainter.

'Stop the car, please.'

The driver jumped slightly from the sudden engagement, obviously lost in his own sour world. He obliged and pulled into an empty spot on the side of the road. Ndumbe slid out of the car and bent over his window. 'Please take my stuff to the address I had put in, neh. You can give them to the security guard at the complex gate. I will add a good tip just to say thanks.'

He nodded, but just in case he changed his mind, she pulled her baby bonsai out through the back window. She cuddled the plant in her arms as she headed into the park.

A gathering of tall trees tickled the clouds above. They were mostly wispy, sparsely-leaved trees with patches of stripped-back bark that made them look like they had large birthmarks. But here and there were trees with thicker trunks and full leaves. These cast cool shades across the park. Ndumbe wound through the park, her steps crackling over branches and leaves as she walked. A soft breeze sent shivers through the park, slightly bending the thin trees and spilling leaves from the others. The bonsai in Ndumbe's arms lifted her short branches, almost as if to embrace her taller counterparts. A leaf at the very top of her branches fluttered up—a lifted head— and bowed with the fading wind, falling to the ground below.

They, Ndumbe and her bonsai, stepped into the lower end of the park, an open, circular, and grassy field dome with shady trees lining the border. Dogs sprinted across the field, frolicked about in the grass, and skulked beneath trees. Ndumbe rounded the outer edge of the dome, eyeing an empty bench beneath a crooked acacia tree. A petite, furry pup came sniffing at her feet, and she resisted the urge to nudge her away. Dogs weren't her thing. Actually, pets weren't her thing. The only living things she ever wanted to be responsible for were her plants and herself. She smiled gingerly as she remembered how just the other day Zola had mocked her for not having given the bonsai a name. 'Seriously, how long have you had this thing for mara Ndumbe, and you still haven't given it a name?'

Ndumbe had first railed Zola for calling her precious baby an 'it' before explaining that she was certain the bonsai would tell her what name she wanted when she was ready. Zola had rolled her big eyes and teased, 'And you say you're *not* a hippy?' The licking pup's owner smiled her apologies, calling to her pet in a sing-song voice, 'Tjommie.' But Tjommie continued to sniff circles around Ndumbe, sticking their snout between her feet until she and her nameless baby arrived at their destination. Ndumbe gently placed the plant onto the bench before dusting off some leaves and soil and lowering herself down too. For the first time that morning—and it was still morning, although it felt like days since she had flustered back to life from the boardroom floor—she listened to her body.

She stretched her long limbs out in front of the bench, pushing her shoes off and digging her toes and heels into the ground. Laying her purse next to her, she curved her back in and out, cat and cow, before spreading it across the back of the bench, paying mind to the tingling pain snaking up and down her spine. Finally, she shut her eyes and pushed through the red sunlight behind her eyelids to the thrum in her forehead. It bopped against the rhythm of her heartbeat and breath, all three merging into a deep mumble. *What are you telling me?* she probed, holding her breath in anticipation of an answer.

Nothing.

'Nothing,' she said to herself and her leafy companion, 'Nothing but a headache, back pain, and some casual blacking out.' Her stomach grumbled, 'And that, too.' Turning to her purse, she rifled through it, pulling out receipts and other papers in search of a snack. At the bottom of the bag, she found a mango fruit roll she could not remember stuffing in there. Sell-by-date: two weeks ago.

'Well, it's barely past the five-second rule for sell-by-dates, neh?'

The bonsai simply stared blankly at her, still and judgemental in the absence of wind. Squinting her eyes in contempt, Ndumbe chomped off a big chunk of the dried fruit. She chewed quickly, trying but failing not to think about that expiry date. *Not bad.*

Ndumbe went in for her second bite, her ravenous jaws split wide like a lion's. Just as she was about to clamp down on the roll, a man appeared around one of the trees, tottering slowly along the pathway. She watched him chuckle at her embarrassment and shake his head at her attempt to quieten her bite into a more delicate nibble.

If her heart hadn't already been thumping furiously all morning, she was sure she would have passed out again just from the sheer embarrassment she felt. To make matters worse, he was making his way toward her with a teasing grin on his face.

Thirty seconds? A minute? She tried to work out the time it would take to slip on her shoes, stuff the leftover snack down her throat, and speed off into a pit. But—sure, the man was slow, old, and reliant on a cane—but she would never get away in time. It was less than a minute before he stood in front of her, eyes gleaming in the sunlight and with humour.

'Sawubona, Nkosazana.'

The gentle familiarity in his voice shocked Ndumbe. It stroked the embarrassment away, inviting her to return his warm smile. 'Sawubona, baba,' Ndumbe greeted back. His thick afro was combed through and patted down, neat as the rest of his clothing. He wore a charcoal, woolly jersey, light brown corduroy pants, and a well-ironed beige shirt. His brown shoes shone as they caught the light. Raising his cane, he tapped on the empty bit of bench next to the baby, 'Can I join your meal?'

Ndumbe giggled unexpectedly, surprised by this gentle old man who could make her laugh after the day—no, the month—she was having. Although there was still laughter in his eyes and the lines around his mouth told of a habit of humour, she did not feel mocked or judged by him. Nor did she feel like he was imposing even though she wanted to be alone. He even waited patiently for her to respond to his request, 'Yes, of course, you can sit.'

The old man hung his cane over the back of the bench. He unhooked a small brown leather bag from his shoulder, clasping it in his lap as he plonked down with a sigh. It took some moving about, a backstretch, and a slow crossing of one knee over the other before he was settled in.

Ndumbe could hear his breathing ease into a slow tune once he was comfortable. She fiddled with the remainder of her snack, unsure what to say now that the greetings had passed. He, on the other hand, seemed relaxed as ever, his eyes shut against the sun, palms resting in his lap. As he sat there, face slightly turned up to the sky, like a flower to the sunlight, Ndumbe found a yearning feeling in her stomach. It was a small tickle at first but slowly scratched at her the longer she watched him. What was her body saying today? What was it trying to tell her?

'What is it, Nkosazana?'

When did you stop looking? When had she stopped looking at him?

'Where did you go?' he asked, still with his eyes closed.

Stripped bits of the mango roll lay in Ndumbe's lap. She'd lost herself looking at him, gnawing at the envious feeling his peace had brought about in her. So gone was she that her hands had decided to come alive on their own in her absence, picking at the snack. Tearing it. Ripping the fleshy rubber bits to shreds.

Again, he waited awhile for her to answer before peeling his eyelids open. 'Tell me, then, since you are not sure where you went just then, how are you today?'

Tears prickled behind her eyelids for the first time that day. She didn't know where to start telling this man, this gentle, old comfort of a man, about her day. About how she'd woken up with a heavy mountain on her chest, but a heart as empty as a cave. What could she tell him of the needling she'd felt in her head as she downed her morning tea and even on her way to work? She wanted to tell him how she arrived at the office and almost collapsed from nausea at the front door. That a snake slithered up from her coccyx right to her temple, moving its tail around to the front of her body and jabbing it into her gut. In the boardroom, when she stood to give her weekly report, the weighty reptile had reared its troublesome head and moved with such speed inside her that it knocked her off her feet. How could she explain that she had a snake coiled in her chest now, passive but hungry? That it been months or more since she'd felt like herself?

She couldn't. Even though his eyes welcomed it, she just couldn't. So, instead, she let the tears leak down to her neck. Without a word or a sound, she wept. She wept for so long that the tears dried up, but she continued the emptying, tugging motion of weeping. He and her bonsai watched her cry, and she let them. The wind came and went, and the sun waved a bright beam through a passing cloud. Even for them, she cried. A group of walkers edged past their bench, wary of this man and tree who sat watching a woman cry. Eyes shut by her sobs, she heard them whisper with concern which made her chuckle through her tears. A desperate chuckle that bubbled into a gross, wet, snotty laugh. She dashed some of her tears away as she laughed, lifting her head up to sunlight, throwing it all the way back, and looking through the leaves of the acacia tree above them.

When she was all spent, the old man reached into his small bag and handed her a carefully folded white handkerchief.

'Thank you.' She smiled.

He nodded his pleasure.

By now, the park around them was blustering with a different life as school children strolled through it on their way home from school. The sun had also begun its descent, casting long, skinny shadows through the trees and shedding an amber glow that coloured the park's world.

The old man stared thoughtfully at the sun before announcing regretfully, 'Soon, I will have to go.'

Slightly disappointed and hoping to prolong their meeting,

Ndumbe questioned, 'Where do you live, baba? Maybe we could walk together?'

A bird let out a hearty twitter somewhere above them, as though chiming the end of their time. At this, the old man smiled. 'Oh, Nkosazana. I was only here to visit umntanam. The child of one of my children, if I must say. Where I live is not a place near here.'

Ndumbe nodded, understanding yet longing to spend more time with this quiet man. They sat in silence, listening to the chatter of the school children, the cheer of the lounging dogs, and the announcements of the birds. When the sun exchanged its amber for a deep orange, he gestured to Ndumbe to pass him his cane. She handed it to him, and he began a rising ritual. He uncrossed his legs and stretched his back and arms once again. He tapped his cane on the ground a few times before trusting it to hold him as he stood. Without a word, he bowed his head and turned back in the direction he'd come from. Ndumbe watched him disappear into the distance, tottering on his cane. Only when she could no longer see him did she turn to look back at their bench, and only then did she see the small leather bag lying beside her bonsai.

Ndumbe picked it up, admiring the golden button on the front before opening it. Inside it, there was a single folded piece of paper and nothing else. Ndumbe pulled the paper out and unfolded it. In a careful handwriting, as quiet and tentative as its owner, the note read, 'Nkosazana. Do not be afraid. I am proud of you, mntanam.'

HELL MERRY
Obinna Obioma

All the gods, all the heavens, all the hells are within you.
Joseph Campbell

Clutching our rosaries, some of us half-heartedly, we kneel around the centre table and listen to Father warm up to his gossip with God. This is what morning devotion on Saturdays has come to be—the perfect time to regale heaven with the atrocities of man. Whatever makes the gist surely does not include the actions of he who alone is eligible to take our supplications to the throne of grace. Heaven profiles him as the pious principal of Perfect Peace School, catechist of St. Peter's Catholic Parish, Nnewi, head and infallible father of the Rapuluchukwus. With these credentials, he breaks the quietude of the hour in lamentation, interceding for the sins of the frail beings that make up his home: Mother, Kamsi, me.

Mother louds her responses. Kamsi yawns and chews. I brace myself for the revelation to come. Father is a bit secretive in his prayers, which is quite unusual. Few teasers, no spoilers. Whatever his mouth is finding so heavy to spill surely must be tasking his soul.

Amen.

We rise and proceed to read from the scriptures. On nights our parents had had a *small* scuffle, the morning reading would be from *Ephesians 5: 22*. Father would rant about the submissiveness of a wife to her husband, the head. Meanwhile, the courts of heaven would hear nothing of whatever it was that made Mother whimper all night long in their bedroom upstairs. Mother herself would make no such appeal. She'd learnt to nurse her scars in silence and to cover her husband's nakedness with parchments of her battered skin.

Today, however, the reading is from *2 Timothy 2: 22*, something on youthful lust, nothing I presume concerns Mother, considering how frantically she leafs through the dog-eared pages of her New King James Bible. I glance at Kamsi huddled up on the settee across. *What have you done?* She rolls her eyes. *Who cares?* I don't, actually. But our parents do—Father mostly, for fear of falling short in his calling and service to the church.

'What kind of a catechist would I be if I don't rule my children and house in the same righteousness and charity I preach?'

Mother, on the other hand, cannot begin to imagine what the other women in her charismatic ministry would say if and when they heard 'that my daughter has sinful video on her phone and dances naked on Instagram? *Chineke ekwela njọ*—God forbid! Kamsiyochukwu, is this what you want to do with your life? This is not how I raised you! Who taught you all these things, eh? Why can't you just emulate your sister, eh?'

That, right there, is the *other* problem: everyone thinking I am Prophetess Anna—the one we read about in the *Nunc Dimittis*—incarnate. Perhaps, the translation of my name, Kosisochukwu, suggests that I am forever covenanted to do *as it pleases God*, as long as life lasts. Well, am I? I've just turned twenty, barely a year older than my sister. While she's the sunny one, more beautifully endowed and patronised by the boys in school, street, or social media, I am the one who keeps the stalkers at bay.

For Mother, my bland attitude is just the right antidote to those 'exuberant, hormonally imbalanced juveniles'. In fact, I am on the straight path to heaven. She couldn't have been more right, only that the truth is I find no paradise in masculine bodies. And *that* is the good problem I needed everyone to find out for themselves, at the peril of their emotions and opinions.

Amen.

Father passes his verdict: Kamsi must go for confession by evening and cleanse her soul in readiness for tomorrow's Mass. She must take communion too, something we just hadn't done since the week of our first communion five years ago, when we lipped the wafers and kissed the goblet of communion. If it becomes necessary, Father threatens he will force-hold my errant sister during Mass and help the priest shove the entire blood and body of Christ down her throat.

Hours later, walking down the hallway, I poke my head through Kamsi's door. 'You'll do it, won't you? It's almost 4 p.m.'

Leaning back on her bed rest, she shifts her gaze from her android phone, barely moving her head. 'Do what?'

'See the priest.'

Her frown relaxes, and her visage glistens with what's left of the facial scrub from hours ago. 'Of course, I'll see the priest. I've been wanting to.'

'Really? That bad? You'd tell him?'

'That I rub my clit every night over some porno? Yeah. It's nothing he's never heard.'

Underlying the tinge of sarcasm is an undecidedly hollow tremor I know so well to be Kamsi being excited. About what? Confession? I do not want to sound abashedly naïve about the next thing I want to ask: *How does it feel—the clit thingy?* I mean, I'm the older one, right? Should have had a taste of the world some full three hundred and sixty-something days before she drew her first breath. But here I am, struggling to keep up with her flippancy and social savviness. I withdraw my head and drift, as I am wont to, away from any further discussions.

In Mother's words, Kamsi is a moral shipwreck, a stubborn she-goat, but an utterly easy-going diva, totally unlike me. If breasts were brains, she'd be a genius, and I'd be Albert Einstein's housemaid. *Did he need any?* I want to think those two heaps of beauty are behind my attraction to girls. At 14, I'd palmed the watermelons already crowding her chest when all I boasted were two shy tangerines. She'd fallen into my arms during one of those awkward teen games that started with boys chasing shadows and girls running from ghosts—everyone mostly heading into a bush of sorts to act 'daddy and mummy'.

Usually, I'd team up with the boys, do the chasing—because I ran from nothing. I'd role-play 'daddy' because mummies got to cook with discarded tins of Gino tomatoes and bathe their 'babies' in the muddy puddles dotting the compound. Daddies, the real deal, moulded mansions out of the wet sands of rainy season—and oh, how I loved to build. The first time, a decade ago, I said to Mother, 'I'm going to build a big house when I become a very big man,' she glared at me, wondering where the misconception had come from. 'Kosisochukwu, you can't be a *man*. You *are* a woman, and you *will* marry a very big man, you hear?'

Back then, her words had greeted me with confusion. What difference did sexual inclination and identity make to a ten-year-old? Now, however, it does. It sounds funny—to think I'd get wooed, asked out, married. I want to do all of those: woo, build my relationship, marry. And since the guys around consider themselves the builders of relationships, I find their advances as disgusting as I find them unattractive. Each time one tries, I feel like I'm being propositioned by a toothless man my grandfather's age. And the thoughts of being wooed lacked the suppleness of Kamsi or the feminine grace of my crush.

Mary. That's her name, my heartthrob. When you sing psalms and solos with a soprano that makes the angelic choir jealous, that strikes their chords of discord because you remind them of Lucifer, their fallen maestro, everyone would know your name, love you, adore you.

Dear Mary,

Why does your voice draw like okra soup? Won't you let me taste God on your sweet lips, worship him at your beauteous feet? No. You're not a great dresser, and I'm not a poet, either. I'm just another pair of ogling eyes that want to strip you, fabric by fabric, reveal the assets you seem so dearly to want to hide from earth's view in those lengthy dresses and choir robes. I am another jittery coward because I can't even ask you out, cos, God, you're 'nun' of what I imagine. Like the ones before it, I'm trashing this letter before it crumples into your palm.

After two years of cooing Mary's name in the dark, I remain tongue-tied, held captive by my sense of propriety. I had these feelings of guilt that I was sexually objectifying her. In the secret carbuncles of my heart, I'd been treating her as though she were Mary of Magda, when in the actual sense, she was Our Lady of Perpetual in the flesh. *Shame on you, Kosi! You'll die a celibate in a Magdalene asylum. This is not the love life you envisioned for yourself. See how your sister is living her dreams, flaunting her big bum-bum and mistakes in the eyes of the world with the impudence of an overpriced peacock.*

Where Kamsi is the kind of girl who'd walk up to a guy and say, *'Hey, can I borrow your penis for a minute?'* I am the kind that can't *man* up to a girl and say, *'Hello, I like you. Do you swing my way?'* Each time I try, my salivary gland secretes adhesives, gumming my mouth shut, and I squirm like the Virgin the first time Gabriel hurtled down to earth to sing, 'Oh favoured blessedness, do you do holy spirits?'

No. Not in these days of cyberbullying. Such annunciations come with a gust of dusty wind. Hit any windpipe the wrong way, and you're spreading all over town on the slobbery mouths of rumourmongers.

Father mounts the pulpit after service today and croaks to everyone's chagrin, 'Satan visited my home in the guise of a reckless daughter with an unwanted pregnancy. Keep praying for us in your different homes.'

In the ensuing tumult of whispers and murmurings, I search the auditorium for Kamsi. I'm just in time to see her half-running out through the back door. *Oh Father, what have you done?* Where Mother sits, she has the murderous look of one who might smother the sanctimonious husbandman in bed. I doubt she would do such a thing because she sits still on her pew and becomes one with the engraving of the crucified Christ and two criminals on the wall beside her. For the many nights she'd spend mending her broken heart at the feet of the Saviour, I pity her. How much of her spiritual integrity has this very day been tarnished—this woman of faith.

I scuttle after my sister, past a warden haranguing a vaguely familiar girl on why she must not enter the church nor sing with the choir wearing 'this cloak of a scarlet woman'.

'Kamsi!'

Too late. She scoots away on a motorcycle, leaving only a cloud of dust and disappointment in her wake. It would have been forgivable if Father peddled this news to God *only*. But no. He blew it wide open to half of Nnewi. And I didn't even know! How much of what happens with my sister do I know? Certainly, it is something equivalent to zero times the distance of our separation. Barely a wall between us at home and a mere phone call away at our different campuses, we were like the earth at perihelion, so close to the sun and warmth, yet so cold.

I stand in the February haze, feeling odd. My younger sister has been impregnated by her misadventures, and I'm standing dazed under a cashew tree, looking as hopeless as the parabolic lost coin, at a loss at exactly how lost I am.

'Hey, are you alright?'

It's *scarlet* girl—scratch that. It's Mary of my wildest fantasies. I rid my eyes of the teary blur and give her the once-over. 'Hi. You look different,' I say, for want of something to say. How long has it been since I last saw her, since my first infatuation? Her dress, which I now agree with that good warden, could seduce the holiest of angels and make Lucifer's one-third rebellious success look like a picnic. Someone either must have had *pro tem* disorientation or found a morale booster in the sudden discovery that she could initiate 'Operation Nudity' without fear. The skimpy V-neck *ankara* is the first time she isn't draped in anything drab and never-in-vogue. It clings to her body as though it fears being tugged off by a force greater than the wearer's will.

'I know, right?'

My lips zip. I nod.

'Hey, you'll be fine. I know your sister; she's my friend in school. I know she's strong too. And she'll be fine.'

'Thank you.'

I'm glad she's offering her moral support despite the embarrassing altercation with the door warden. I want to make more conversations now that my wet dream was standing merely two feet away, with perked-up busts ready to be devoured.

'Do you want to go sit somewhere and talk?' Mary lets a small smile part her glossy lips.

I panic. 'Umm. Would love to. But I have to head home now.'

'Alright. I'll see you around then. Kosi, right?'

'Yes,' I confirm.

'Okay. Call me.' She nods quaintly and sashays away, her skirt creasing with each stride, revealing newer inches of smooth velvety thighs. Inside, the church sings Blest Be the Ties that Bind, in dismissal of what would be the cloudiest day in the history of the Rapuluchukwus, or not.

I don't want to think that Mary's been mistaken to assume I had her number. This was not how I imagined our first real meeting (church vicinity or yes). *She is going to be your girlfriend, and nothing is going to stop you. You are supposed to be all over her, Kosi. Dominant. Not dormant. Wooing her!*

When I get home, partly fuming at myself, Mother surprisingly is fanning a bigger fire, in the sitting room, beside the centre table, our makeshift altar. 'For the first time, you just couldn't cover our sins. You had to strip us of our honour in public—'

Father retorts, 'It is the relatives of a madman that feel shame. You spoilt her. You!'

'I did? I did? You think you could have caged her better? What good has flagellating me every time for her misbehaviour done for you? Whip me now. I say, flog me! We will all burn in Hell, me, my daughters, and your self-righteous ass. This family will roast in Hell!'

She flings herself at him. I lunge at her before she could tear at the obviously petrified man.

'*Álá ayịgokwa nne-i.*' He smirks at me.

'It's you who's raving mad. Tell me, what man in his right senses would force himself into his unwilling wife every night and make her cry, so he rides on her pains? Do I go about with megaphone screaming to the world that that's the only way you enjoy sex? No! *Ị ịụlụ taa,* you must tar the road that leads to Cathedral with our burnt ashes. Kosisochukwu, leave me, let me deal with this monster!'

I do not let her go. I cling to her, holding her tighter than ever.

She's awash with hysteria. I hope she doesn't lose her mind or let this newfound fire of revolution engulf her. I hope it's not true that those nights before we wake up to Paul's letter to the Ephesians, Father flogs her for Kamsi's misdeed and, while at it, leaves the imprints of his sadistic libido between her legs.

Kamsi comes out of her room, dragging an Ecolac bag, wearing a blue tank top and a bittersweet grin. She must go away to live with our aunt in Asaba until the storm passes, until she puts to bed and is delivered of the demon growing inside her.

'Kamsi, go back inside. You go nowhere,' Mother barks.

'I'll murder you both if this lousy harlot spends a minute more here,' Father growls. The quarrel intensifies. I let go of Mother and run to meet my sister outside.

'Who's responsible, do you know?'

Her eyes linger on a brown lizard basking in the afternoon sun across the veranda before they return to look into mine with a deep sigh. 'It's the priest.'

'The priest? At the parish?'

'Yup. We've been seeing since that confession Father forced me to make. Do you know he drives down to my school on Friday nights and leaves by morning? He's a sweet man. You don't know the implement he hides under that cassock. You don't.' She laughs, a mirthless laugh that pulverises in the heat of noon. I cup my mouth to stop myself from screaming.

'Oh, please, they're humans. They have erections too. Do you know that that first confession, he was quite interested in the details? He forgave me, advised sixty-nine recitals of *Hail Mary*. It didn't work. I went back the next Saturday, met him at the vestry to tell him I was the porn girl. He offered to absolve me of my sins himself, and I won't say he's not been doing a good job this past year.'

We giggle in spite of ourselves. 'He's not supposed to know the penitent.'

'Well—'

'You've been crushing on him.' I finish for her in sudden realisation.

Kamsi blushes, a similitude to the expression that pervaded her face the first time she talked about the priest in her room. I confirm that she's as crazy as she's smitten.

'Father offered me the perfect opportunity to be with him. And here I am, carrying his anointed baby. But hey, don't tell anyone until I sort it all out. He's afraid. Shit wasn't supposed to happen, not like this anyway. Now, he's planning to quit the priesthood and—'

'Oh, Kamsi,' I hug her. 'I don't know what to think. But I hope he comes around and takes care of you.'

When we finally let go of ourselves, Kamsi says, 'You are not totally a saint, you know? I know you're into girls. You just be careful when you're ready to explore. There's little light out there for your kind.'

My mind flashes to a video clip tagged exorcism, making the rounds on Instagram. It is of a pretty teen girl and her partner, of kisses, cuddling, and photographed orgasms in the privacy of a hotel room, of her siblings stumbling on the love story, getting a hold of her and flexing their big-brother fists all over her body. When they are done, their father gets his turn at pummeling her, screaming into her face, 'You demon of a girl, don't you know me? Don't you know this family?' She weeps, the poor girl. Her mother, akimbo, stands aside, watching the lynching of her 'only daughter'. Everyone—online and offline—got their pound of the flesh of the possessed girl who'd brought shame to her family. I dwell on this for a minute, cold shivers shuttling down my spine.

Kamsi hugs me again and squeezes a piece of paper into my hand.

I ball my palm into a fist as she walks gingerly away to a waiting bike-man, leaving me to battle my tears and confusion.

That night, alone in bed, I cry myself to sleep. Around midnight, I rise with knee-jerk sobriety to check the piece of paper that reminds me of my sister's departure. I'd almost forgotten about it. I unfold it to find it is the ode to an old love, renewed. *Dear Mary.* Somehow, Kamsi had found my fear, archived it, done me the honours of mailing it 'To Whom It May Concern', and the reply had come, written on the other side of the rumpled sheet of two years ago. *I love you too, Kosi. Call me.* A hasty scribble. My heart dances to the beat of Andrea Boccelli's 'Funiculi Funicula', played with the ecstatic tempo of highlife. I dial the number. She knew I'd call, like she knew I had her number.

'I got your message, Kosi,' her singsong voice rings out without the initial strains of prevarication or sleepiness.

'I got yours, too.'

'Can you come to my place?'

'Tomorrow?'

'Whenever.'

'Alright.'

Once my mind's eye searches and stays on her cleavage from earlier in the day, and my nipples grow the right amount of taut, I slip my left palm downstairs and tease myself for the first time. The imageries of my mental torture switch from Kamsi's slender figurine to Mary's chocolatey frame, the searing sweetness between my legs needing vent.

I get to her place after missing my way twice, two evenings later. She lives alone in a self-contained room. She is by the door playing the piccolo. I pick the tunes: *What child is this, who laid to rest, on Mary's lap is sleeping?*

'Can you sing along?' she pleads. 'I want to hear what your singing voice sounds like.'

'I can't sing.' I don't even want to try, and I'm distracted because she's on the sexiest briefs I'd seen anyone wear.

'Come in. The mosquitoes have finished my legs. You kept me waiting.'

A portrait of a breastfeeding mother hangs from the pink wall. The halo on the infant's head depicts him as divinity. I think of Kamsi and the baby bulging inside of her. I think of me suckling on Mary's lap. She offers me a seat on her queen-sized bed, Fanta from a tabletop fridge, and sits so close I melt into her body's perfume.

'How long now?'

I'm enmeshed in her aura, engrossed with sipping my drink, that I don't quite get her question. My eyes perhaps say I'm lost, superimposed, owned. She rephrases, 'How long have you been into me?'

I stutter and start all over again. 'Since I first heard you sing in church, I think.'

'And you don't think it's wrong?'

'What's wrong?'

'To love a fellow girl.'

'Do you?'

'Do I what?'

'Love me back?'

'I told you already.'

'Then it's nothing wrong.'

'You're witty.'

She smiles and takes the empty bottle from me.

'Why? What changed?'

'Do you want a requiem on preference and sensuality, or would you like to see?'

'I don't know. Maybe both.'

She frees her boobs from their bra, laughs, and wiggles them in my face.

'Here. You can have *both* now.'

The world thins down to a breathless whisper, moans, flashes of her phone's camera, and more giggles. Six months later, we're still shy to tell God that we're dating, that I am her girlfriend. It sounded too daring, like telling him to his face that we're fornicating and we didn't give two fucks if he roasted our souls in Hell. Nonetheless, someone had to tell him, let the heavens know we found the lost Eden on earth, that in return for peace and satisfaction, I gave her laughter, turned her into a mosquito assassin, and taught her to have a sixth or seventh meal of the day as early or as late as 3 a.m.

The tiding of goodwill is first broken to Facebook patriots when Mary makes a long post and uploads a picture of us kissing passionately in bed. Like an enraged pandemic, it goes viral, and I am ill-prepared for the fiery reactions that follow when a blog headline reads: *Daughter of Catholic Catechist and Ex-chorister Do Lesbian Porno.* Nicely barbecued and peppered-up for the gossip-hungry.

Kamsi video calls from Asaba. 'Big sis, you're making pornos now?' We laugh—her tummy heaves.

'You know that's not true. How's your boyfriend?' I ask.

'He's fine. He was defrocked. He comes to see me as often as he can. Since he tasted the forbidden fruit, he's convinced the celibate life was never for him.'

'Who was it meant for then?'

'Why don't you ask his father who sent him to seminary school in the first place?' She smirks. 'How's your partner?'

'She's unbearably hot. Do you know we're almost age-mates? But with her, I don't mind being owned.' I wink.

It is more than Father and the church can bear. Mother, who now feels twice crucified, wishes I'm like Kamsi—inclined to doing boys. My last night at home, she stares as a neighbour's cockerel runs after an old black layer. 'Kosisochukwu,' she points from the verandah, 'that's the natural order of things. Drop out of school, carry *belle*, mess up your life, anything but this madness.'

Mine is the worst of transgressions, top on the list of unpardonable sins, deserving of excommunication from the local parish and banishment from the fold of God. But what do I care? I want to tell Mother that, growing up, the eleventh commandment had been to stay away from boys. No one said anything about girls. No law, no sin. See? I want to tell her saddened soul that she can only *allow* Father to bind and fuck her in the anus *if* she enjoys it, too. I want to tell Father that he's a hypocritical jackass, that to be Catholic is to be liberal, that Pope Francis himself can wed as many gay or lesbian couples as he wants, hold mass in the shrine of *Amadiọha*, and heaven will only fall when hell freezes over.

I move in with Mary the day after. Before we sleep, she drapes me, head to shoulders, in the *ankara* wrapper we use as a blanket, holds my hands, and prays aloud: *Dear Lord, thank you for the gift of this soul. Bless her immensely cos she's my girl officially, and I won't be talking to you right now if it weren't for her. Amen.*

She unveils my face as a groom would, and whispers, 'I may now kiss my bride.' Her lips envelop mine before I blurt a teary laugh.

Next day, I go on Facebook and update my profile: *Lesbian. Tradochrislam. In a relationship.*

MADAM LIEUTENANT JACK
Moses Abukutsa

Congolese rhumba is papa's ghost on his third death anniversary. It has gathered everyone in our house. It has drowned Musa in beer. It distracts me. To steady myself, I pick my cousin Ambiyo's baby. A clock chimes. An old black and white photograph stares down the chime; in its epicentre stands the godfather of many, my grandfather. He is a rod of iron in overalls, leaning on an *East African Railways* locomotive bogie.

My eyes scan the other photographs scattered on the wall. There is this breathing photo; it is Grandmother. She rests on the opposite wall. There is a radiance about her as she sits on grass. The gap between her teeth, the symmetry of her body, the broad hips in a polka-dotted shirtwaist dress, brown comb poking out of her Afro hair. The wind of time has carried away this flower's glow, its petals withering. When I look at her, she is chewing a leaf and smiling. I smile back, enamoured, rocking the bundle of joy in my hands.

'Wasn't I a hibiscus?'

Yes, wasn't she? Ambiyo hands her a cold glass of Fanta Orange, and I push my seat closer to her. I want to drink the nectar of the hibiscus, listen to one of the many stories she pours into our gatherings whenever she remembers what she once was. My eyes go over the East African Railways photograph again. In it, Kuka is handsome and young. His thoughtful eyes and natural smile radiate charm. I see what Kukhu fell for. Bewitching dimples, a kempt moustache, sharp piercing eyes. I see why her favourite seat faces that photo, why she looks at it when she tells her stories. She lost a man she loved with all her heart. She sighs as if agreeing with my thoughts.

'Two daughters. Your kuka wanted two daughters and four sons.'

'And you gave birth to papa and aunty Esseli.'

'Yes. And your kuka, one of the first Quakers, had three brothers. Two died. The one who lived married a wife that your grandfather blamed for everything wrong in his brother's life. Her name was Valentina Sikwa.'

'Grand aunty Sikwa?'

Underneath her sigh is a shadow of memories, a resurrection of fire from dead ashes. A brightened face emerges from this shadow— and chuckles. 'We were like kittens. Your kuka always said he missed the best dancer of *Kalwoto* but found the best cook'. Again, she chuckles, relishing fond memories of those early days of marriage. 'Oh, I married a boastful man.'

On their wedding day, they received gifts from many well-wishers; they even had biscuits and sweets. Kukhu became friends with Sikwa, her sister-in-law and a grain trader. But Kuka's stomach boiled whenever Sikwa was around. He believed she was the reason his brother was childless. Whenever she visited their house, Kuka acted like a man with safari ants in his trousers. He'd fix his eyes on her and bore through everything she touched.

One windy Christmas night, Sikwa and Kuka's brother, Opati, visited. Later that night, pebbles and sand grated my grandparents' iron roof, and a strange fire seared through Kukhu. She woke Kuka up. He sat up on their sisal mattress, staring into the rafters. His pulse was violent, his mind a chaotic market of thoughts. There was some quiet for a few minutes, and then the disquieting grating sounds of pebbles intensified as if encouraged by the few minutes of quietness.

'This spirit is back again.' In a huff, Kuka gathered scattered thoughts into a shirt.

'What spirit?'

'Have you not heard about the spirit Opati's wife brought with her mother's *isiongo*?'

Kukhu stared at him, her chest heaving up and down, foraging for meaning in his words.

'Have you ever asked yourself why my brother is childless?'

'Tell me.'

'Sikwa is a night runner. And she has offered her body to *Esinini*.'

'Offered her body to a spirit?'

'A spirit who is her other husband.'

They muttered a quick prayer. Kuka walked out into the night. He shone a flaming torch around the house, wore a brave face, trusted in a throbbing heart, and waved a King James Version Bible to scare away the disrupter of peace and her malevolent spirit. Before that night, these two fresh converts of the Quakers Friends Church had been living without torment. He went around the house seven times, chanting prayers and reciting crammed bible verses, until in exhaustion, his voice hoarse, he crept back into bed. And though they kept turning and tossing, the rest of the night was calm.

When Sikwa showed up at her kiosk three days later, Kukhu was arranging groceries. As drops of rain splattered on the kiosk's roof, the night of the terrible grating flashed through Kukhu's mind, Kuka's words—'Sikwa is a night runner, and she has offered her body to *Esinini*'—tumbling over each other in her head. Rainwater dripped down Sikwa's dress, now clinging to her body. She huddled into the chair Kukhu offered her, the water from her dress settling on the floor in little puddles. The rain had caught up with her on her way there to get New Year's groceries.

'I don't know which medicine will cure my childlessness?'

'You say medicine, you don't know—'

Sikwa shifted her eyes. Kukhu cleared her throat.

'Who is the issue?'

'You see, the issue cannot be who.'

'But—?'

'People say I, Sikwa, am the issue.'

'Do you not run naked at night?'

'I'm not a night runner. People say those things and more. Some say I came with a spirit in my bridal *isiongo*. Some say I sacrificed my children to spirits. Children I have never had.'

Sikwa caught Kukhu's eyes surveying her face. There was digging and excavation through the rubble of her words in that surveillance.

'It is true I have offered my body to *Esinini*.'

Kukhu squirmed. Behind the kiosk's counter, packets of sugar and salt, a tray of roasted groundnuts, sweets, and loaves of bread on shelves rustled as she reached for a packet of salt and placed it on the counter. The bluntness of her sister-in-law surprised her. Laughter exploded from Sikwa, cutting through the thick air. She grabbed the salt and the rest of the groceries from the counter and stuffed them into her reed basket.

'Esinini?'

Kukhu's interest made her eager to elaborate. 'Yes, a husband from the spirit world, manifesting only to the most beautiful women.'

'You are talking pots and pots of mushroom-poisoned soups. Have you gone mad?'

'Call me pots of mushroom-poisoned soups, but I tell you, his name is Lieutenant Jack, and he is in the British Army of 1945. He enlisted in 1938.

'So spirit husbands are beberus?'

'Mine is a British beberu. I don't know if others are beberus. Maybe. I don't know.'

'This Esinini beberu of yours, how does—?'

'Dreams, in my dreams. I go into his world. When this happens, my body is no longer mine. I open a door, Lieutenant Jack's door. Once my eyes shut, I drift into sleep, and he comes. The first time he came, Opati was a snoring, clammy, limp nakedness beside me. His square shoulders appeared first, then the crew cut and hair that bristled like the mane of a lion in the sun, and then a handsome white face like the photographs of the angels in the Quakers Church Bible Stories book. I fell. And then there was a lit cigarette smouldering between his lips. This was the perfect man.'

'This perfect man, he was smoking that thing which roasts lungs?'

Sikwa nodded. 'He is the handsomest man.'

'Handsomest? Since when have you known how to see the handsome looks of a beberu that is as white as the inside of a cassava peel?'

'In Lieutenant Jack, I have found those eyes. You know my mother lied to me that when they are old, these beberus, they turn red and their skins crease into rough ugly gulleys infested with splotches like those around a turkey's red neck. You know that is elephant shit. You know.'

'I know people say baskets of elephant shit.'

'Baskets of elephant shit, yes. People say many elephant shit things. Yet, Lieutenant Jack. He is no elephant shit. This beberu has made blood run through every part of my body like someone was chasing it with a knife. *Bane!* He has made me hear my heart in my ears. My breasts erect firm, and the river of fire from them flood my head. I stopped reasoning, and Lieutenant Jack, he drew close to make me reason again. Otherwise, I was running mad. His fingers talked the language of my body. I melted. I wanted it. He did it.

Then I woke up. Opati was there. He towered over me, huffing, naked, a bullwhip in his hands, imagine.'

Kuhku imagined. She imagined Opati raging, 'Who is Lieutenant Jack?' Opati must have growled the question like a bulldog, jerking Sikwa into the present. Sikwa had spoken and made revelations unknowingly in her sleep. Opati bullwhiped her. She felt like telling him it was his mess—his lassitude in bed and clammy nakedness—that had driven her to this world of Lieutenant Jack, but she knew better. She muted her protest. Yet, her body remained at the mercy of Lieutenant Jack. He kept coming.

The rain stopped splattering and thinned to a drizzle. Sikwa picked up her groceries, ignoring pleas from Kukhu to wait for the rain to subside even further, and made her way home.

That evening, Valentina Sikwa was the main course on Kukhu and Kuka's dinner table.

'It is true. She has Esinini, and he is a beberu.'

'We must beat prayer drums more than ever before now that I can say *Our Father* in English. She is your *mwalikhwa,* but I warn you, eat not with that sister-in-law of yours ever. A single meal, and you are the fish on the hook. Esinini beberu is very promiscuous.'

'But she comes by the kiosk many times.'

'Keep your eyes open, my wife.'

Three days later, Kukhu's mother died, and Sikwa brought green maize, dry maize, millet, and a live cockerel with a Lieutenant Jack story.

'He is flooding the river of fire in my valley.'

'*Bane!*'

The cockerel cackled. Kukhu clamped its beak with her fingers.

'Last night, he took me to his camp. It is at the foot of a muddy hill infested with mosquitoes. I was excited. Guns rattled as soldiers polished their long barrels and laughed like cracking fire. Some were drunk, some saluted him, others squawked like ducks. He seemed to enjoy it. It was a strange country we were in. It was unbelievable. He took me to his tent, and on a straw mattress, you see, you know, it started again.'

This time Opati had no moderation. He whipped Sikwa to near hallucination. Then he disappeared without a trace. For three years. Kuka counted him as dead. Sikwa never left her home as Kukhu expected. She waited for Opati.

Lieutenant Jack was relentless. He kept coming. On the night before the Hiroshima and Nagasaki atomic bombings, they had their wedding in the camp at the foot of a hill. She glowed in a white silk gown, a bouquet of pink hibiscus flowers cuddled in her arms and a garland of pink and white roses on her hair, straightened and flowing down her shoulders like that of a beberu woman. Soldiers belted smothering acapella renditions of hymns and carols as a priest in a starched white cassock bound the couple in matrimony.

The hill vanished in Lieutenant Jack's fat smile, and she blushed, falling into his arms. She was a thirsty dry rock drinking new rain after ages of barrenness, a black woman in the rain of white faces. Nobody was calling her Negro; she was Madam Lieutenant Jack. They disappeared into his private quarters. She was jittery. He grabbed her by the waist and planted a ferocious kiss on her lips. They danced to the song of new life on the horizon. Her heart galloped like a horse. He was breathing Scotch whisky, kissing her passionately, and fondling her breast roughly like a soldier cocks a rifle. Did she mind? No. She surrendered like the vanished hill, wholeheartedly.

Kuka was snoring beside her when she woke up with a sore breast, his shirt and trousers in a bundle on the floor. She remembered Opati. He was gone. But what did it matter? His brother was here.

The only other time stone and pebbles grated their iron roof, Kuka huffed into a confrontation with Kukhu, 'What is this?'

'What is what?'

'You have become Esinini.'

'Me?'

'Keep your eyes open, my wife. Remember you told me? Huh! Men. I kept them open, husband. So don't pretend with me. You know it is you competing with Esinini beberu.'

'There are very many mad women but surely not my wife collecting garbage from every basket that runs around with stench.'

'You are shameless!'

'You are babbling.'

'Don't raise your voice at me. I'm babbling because you are shameless. You have been putting that thing into Valentina Sikwa from the time your brother disappeared.'

'Now you are vomiting nonsense.'

Kuka let out a deep sigh and, barechested, stormed into the night, flashing a flaming torch. He was guilty, and he knew it. It was this guilt that held back the fist he wanted to throw at Kukhu. His mind whirled with remorse for that adultery. There was only one route to a fresh beginning with Kukhu, and that door opened on New Year's Eve. He got a new job as a locomotive driver, a job he had trained for under an Indian supervisor for six months. Before he left for the job, he confessed and asked Kukhu to forgive his transgression. Out of her abundant love, she forgave him. The job gave him time to reconstruct his life away from the shadow of adultery and a looming dysfunctional marriage.

The end of the war had come with opportunities for people like him who had to fend for young wives, people who wanted to make something out of themselves in the changing times. Stories of men from the war in Burma spread like wildfire among men who had not been to the war. Returnees from Burma who had seen the Lieutenant Jacks of this world fold and die like insects, yet were treated like flies and called *wahuni*. They fermented uprisings, clamoured for freedom. Kuka, as soon as he started working, discretely took part in the liberation movement, incensed by the unforgivable loss of his twin brothers, careful not to lose his new colonial government job, driving the locomotive from Nairobi to Kisumu, which earned him a modest wage of twenty shillings a month. He contributed a fair share of this wage to the underground liberation movement—for assembling homemade guns for the liberators and facilitating the hiring of left-wing propagandists, journalists, and lawyers from London for the great freedom cause. At least that was what the canvasser for the Freedom Fighters Underground Association of North Kavirondo (FFUANK), who kept an inventory of all the supportive and quisling African colonial government workers, told him when he collected his previous month's contribution of five shillings.

Opati returned to Sikwa just before FFUANK was caught napping in 1952, when Sir Evelyn Baring declared a state of emergency. This was several days after Kuka was asked to take a work leave without pay, days that he spent with his old bible. He flew to Opati's house with his bible and took an elevated cowhide chair without being offered. Kukhu stood in the doorway, trying to read the face, under dishevelled locks of kinky hair, of the pregnant woman with Opati. Sikwa couldn't find the composure to sit in her own house. She kept sneering and blowing her nose into a worn headscarf, assessing the pregnant intruder.

'What is this nonsense, Opati?'

'This nonsense is my second wife.'

'This thing?'

'I'll cut that sharp tongue out if you continue insulting my decision.'

'Surely love potions have made cows from men. Their feet have been dragged to the doors of strange women.'

'Who are you calling strange women? It was your husband who came to a widow's bed. Mine was a hero who died in the war. You didn't do it properly. You were busy doing it with another thing, childless hen, Ptho!'

'I'll make this whore drink my urine!'

'Whore is you.'

'Let's be calm.'

'Let me be.' Sikwa attempted to free herself from Kukhu's iron clasp around her waist, but realising the futility of fighting a stout taller woman, she stopped.

'How can I be calm? I'm falling into pieces of pain and madness. Opati disappears and reappears, and then a thing appears with an anthill, claiming my husband, saying he pumped the anthill into her.'

'I'm a man, and I will pump anthills wherever I want.'

'That is the spirit of adultery speaking. Beware and guard that well from which issues of life sprout.' Kuka's reprimand drops from his self-appointed chair in an even and flat voice.

'You should guard your trousers first, mister. Keep the buttons tucked bottom-up, Brother Christian,' Opati chuckles and spits. 'The holy one who sleeps with his brother's wife when his brother is away. You are not my brother. I disown you. I excommunicate you. Leave my house. I have no doubt you have been Lieutenant Jack all these years.'

'He is a good man.'

'Good Man Lieutenant Jack is so good that he worships in the temple of your thighs.'

'Opati, that tongue will destroy you!'

'The death of the tongue is more honourable than death between thighs.'

'You have left your head, my brother.' Kuka shifts uncomfortably in the chair, aggrieved, his anger almost bursting the seams of his restraint.

'I see how you are in yours, ex-brother. The excellent head of a man like you who fucks people's wives. Let's do justice and cut cut our wives into half half.'

'You are mad.'

'Since I am mad, and you are not willing to get out, I will leave with my madness.' Opati grabbed the pregnant woman, who chuckled in triumph, the tap-tap of their feet fading into the gathering darkness.

Kuka was stunned. It was Kukhu who unstunned him. She unclasped her arms from Sikwa's waist, heaved Kuka from the chair, and led him out.

Opati disappeared again. Sikwa floundered on the night of his disappearance. When she went to sleep, she was alone. Lieutenant Jack did not show up. Her body couldn't hold sleep. She was hollow. Later that night, she saw him pick a rifle and blast his brains: there was no suicide note. He had shot himself after wrestling with PTSD. His soldiers buried him in an unmarked grave. She woke up at midnight alone, floating in a tunnel of darkness, groping for invisible walls. She decided she should go after Lieutenant Jack.

In the darkness, she reached for her mother's *isiongo*, the pot prepared by mothers for their daughters when they are betrothed, the one which had been suspected of holding a strange spirit within it. Lifting it, she smashed the sacredness on the earthen floor so violently that it was reduced to smithereens. A sigh broke from her throat. Tears stung her eyes. The strange musty stench from the stained clothes of the pregnant woman and her dishevelled kinky hair lingered in her memory: she hardly knew her name, the name of her adversary, the present tormentor of her hollowness, the one who finally made her husband a man. The tears that stung her eyes flowed freely like rain escaping the gates of heaven. She groaned, prostrate on their matrimonial bed. With effort, she clambered on heavy limbs to the corner of the room, where there was a stool and a rusty toolbox. She dragged the stool to the part of the wall with a twined sisal rope held by two nails adjacent to each other. The rope was for hanging their clothes. She climbed on the stool and clawed the nails out of the wattle using a rusty hammer. The clothes slumped, and Lieutenant Jack's blown brains flashed in her head. She discarded the hammer, dragged the stool close to her bed and got on it again. She tied one end of the rope to the rafter above the bed and then made a knot around her neck. Opati, the pregnant woman, Kukhu, Kuka, and Lieutenant Jack were not with her. The uninfringeable darkness that swallows souls drew her into its belly.

'So Grand Aunty Sikwa killed herself because she was childless?' My head is lighter than my voice as I emerge from the other end of the tunnel of darkness that aunty Sikwa dissolves in, through the door of Kukhu's eyes, back into the sitting room, my eyes still traipsing the photographs on the scarred walls.

'That is how Madam Lieutenant Jack died, a few years before true independence.' Kukhu's voice is dry. The words bounce onto the black and white photographs. She quaffs the now warm Fanta Orange.

The late afternoon, sluggish in its suffocating heat, draws everyone into the repose of momentary silence. Musa, exhausted from beer and rhumba, slumps into a sofa. Papa's ghost is now silent, and beer bottles are empty. Aunty Esseli takes the baby from my hands, and mama takes it from her. I scrutinise Kukhu's photograph one last time. It is how I imagine Queen Sheba on her pilgrimage to Solomon, the kind of image that makes you write that one who conquers a soul is better than one who conquers a city. My eyes dart back to her, happy to see her babble with excitement under the shade of her family tree. Her bony hands and the canvas of skin around them ripple with pleasure as my other cousins from Nairobi arrive, late. They are the other story better left untold. She has read my mind.

THE AUTHORS

Okwubi Godwin Adah is a Nigerian writer. He is the winner of the Nigerian Students Poetry Prize 2020 (NSPP, 2020) and has works appearing in Iskanchi Press and the Poets in Nigeria (PIN) anthology. He has been longlisted for the Afritondo Short Story Prize 2022. He enjoys reading Cormac McCarthy and Imbolo Mbue. You can find him on Twitter and Instagram @ goddy_adah .

Somto Ihezue is an Igbo writer, filmmaker, and wildlife enthusiast. A Nommo Award nominee and winner of the African Youth Network Movement Fiction Contest, his works have appeared or are forthcoming in Tordotcom: Africa Risen Anthology, Fireside Magazine, Omenana Magazine, Cossmass Infinities, OnSpec Magazine, The 2021 Year's Best Anthology of African Speculative Fiction, Ibua Journal, Africa In Dialogue, and others. He is an associate editor at Cast of Wonders and tweets @somto_Ihezue. He has a dog, River, and two cats, Salem and Ify.

Lynsey Ebony Chutel is a writer and journalist living in Johannesburg, South Africa. As a journalist, she covers a continent in flux, through the lens of politics, culture, gender and climate. She has travelled through more than a dozen African countries as a reporter. As a fiction writer, Lynsey Ebony is comfortable with admitting that she is still finding her voice, and is both terrified and exhilarated by the prospect that this may be a lifelong search.

Her essays on the historical and contemporary identity of South Africa's descendants of the enslaved and indigenous people, known as Coloured South Africa, will appear in the forthcoming book Coloured: How Classification became Culture (published by Jonathan Ball). Her fiction has appeared in the literary journal Pank and her still evolving debut novel was shortlisted for the Miles Morland Foundation Writing Scholarship.

Raheem Omeiza is a first-class graduate of Agriculture from the University of Ilorin, Nigeria where he majored in Agricultural Economics. His works are published or forthcoming in The Story Tree Challenge Maiden Anthology, Afritondo and elsewhere. His works explore boyhood, grief, sexuality and the liminal spaces where they intersect. Raheem Omeiza is Ebira and writes from Lagos, Nigeria. He tweets @raheem_omeiza on Twitter.

Sabah Carrim has authored two novels, and her shorter work has been selected in a variety of international competitions, namely the AfroYoung Adult Short Story Competition, Bristol Short Story Prize, Not-So-Normal-Narrators contest, Gabriele Rico Challenge for Creative Nonfiction and the Small Islands Anthology Contest. She has a PhD in Genocide Studies and was awarded the W. Morgan and Lou Claire Rose Fellowship for an MFA in Creative Writing in the United States.

Howard Meh-Buh Maximus is a Cameroonian writer and scientist. His work has appeared in anthologies as well as literary magazines. He is a winner of the Miles Morland Scholarship 2020, Kalahari Short Story Prize (2), and a semi-finalist for the Alpines Fellowship 2019. He is an awardee of the W. Morgan and Lou Claire Rose Fellowship, currently studying for an MFA in Fiction.

Mazpa Ejikem (he/him) survives in Nigeria, one day at a time. He is an award-winning physician and writer. His works have won the ALITFEST21 Prize for Short Stories, Collins Elesiro Prize for Fiction, and LIPFEST prize for Poetry among several other recognitions.
He describes himself as unapologetically content and willfully childish. You may follow him on Instagram and Twitter @mazpa_md

Bwanga 'Benny Blow' Kapumpa has been trying to publish a novel since he was eight. He would staple A4 paper in half, scribble new worlds between pages, and illustrate his covers. He is from Lusaka, Zambia.

He put his novelist aspirations on hold for years, studying to be a chartered accountant and blogging while grappling with imposter syndrome, until his short story, The Wandering Festival, was published in the AKO Caine Prize for African Writing's anthology in 2016. He was shortlisted for the Miles Morland Foundation Scholarship in 2020 and 2021.

In 2020, Bwanga diversified his work and has been learning about conceptual art with the Livingstone Office for Contemporary Art.

Working as a freelance writer puts food on his table and affords him reasonably priced beer.

Bwanga is trying to tell more Zambian stories, inspired by folklore and any stranger-than-fiction real-life events. He hopes to inspire others to use their imagination.

Jocelyn Fryer, having majored in a masters in English Literature, is finally trying to find the words to bring to light the causes close to her heart.

It is so far an eclectic collection of writing it can be said, from reframing conversations around mental health matters, being diagnosed and hospitalised at the age of 29 with bipolar disorder, to rescuing forgotten folklore and female heroines of literary days gone by, her curiosities and interests are vast. But always, she believes, she invests in stories that need telling, stories that need some hope. Her blog, www.myhumblepie.co.za, is a space for all her whims and wishes.

And at the ripe 'old' age of 37, she has begun to try her hand full time at fiction, besides her blogging, to tell her story in all its guises, a story made of many stories of recovery, a story of suffering, but also, of joy. Hope. Beyond this, in the fiction she writes now, wiser, she seeks to distil the marvels, the wonders, in even the very most ordinary. Recently, she published her first novella, Zimmer, on Amazon Kindle.

You can otherwise find her either barefoot in the kitchen or advocating the adoption of stray animals. That is, when she's not battling the thorn in her side that is white heteronormative patriarchy or stigmas. Other times you'll find her at her best, enjoying a patch of grass by the wildflowers.

Follow her on @FryerJocelyn on Twitter, or alternatively, with her other 'book baby': @bookendsportalfred on Instagram

Finally, merrily feel free to befriend her on Facebook: Jocelyn Teri Fryer (for a curated experience of all her passions, a veritable rabbit hole to get lost down!)

Victor Ola-Matthew is a Nigerian storyteller—films, screenplays, stage plays, prose, but no dancing—currently residing in Toronto, Ontario. A 2019 Quramo Junior Writers' Prize finalist, his short story You, Me and Philadelphia appears in the debut issue of Cape Town-based literary magazine, Everyday Journal.

Efua Boadu is a British-Ghanaian writer and educator. She is currently completing an MA in Creative Writing in North-West England. In early 2019, her poetry was shortlisted for the Palette poetry Emerging Poet Prize.

She also recently made the final fifteen shortlist to join Southbank's New Poetry Collective. One of her short stories, A Good View, has been published on Afritondo, along with a poem, Okukor. She tweets @FRH210 and blogs at efuaboadu.com.

Alain Patrick Irere Hirwa is a Kigali-based communications guy who writes, among other things. He had a very religious upbringing, which gave him the audacity to get creative with spirituality through his writing, in an attempt to find answers to meagerly formulated questions. If he isn't sitting in a boring office, with headsets on, typing at a questionably slow speed for someone who wants to be a writer, you can always find him with a small camera in his hands, chasing some cool shot of coffee cherries in the rural area. Nyabingi is Awake is Alain Patrick's first short story.

Alex Kadiri writes from Lagos, Nigeria. He is a graduate of English and Literary Studies and has been longlisted/shortlisted for Stories of the Nature of Cities, Koffi Addo Prize for Nonfiction, Awele Creative Trust, Problem House Press etc. He has contributed fiction at ShortSharpShort, WordsAreWork, Whipik and Afreada.

He was the winner of the Quramo Writers' Prize 2020 and is the author of Sunshower, a product of his award-winning manuscript. When he is not stringing words for make-believe worlds, Alex divides his time between binge-watching movies and reading quality fiction. Other times, he challenges people from around the world at chess or just goes swimming. Find him on Instagram via @alexwrites

Uvile Memory Samkelisiwe Ximba is a writer and creative practitioner. She completed her Bachelor of Arts Honours in Politics and International Relations and Dramatic Arts. She was selected as an ASSITEJ South Africa 'In The Works' 2020 playwright, and worked as an intern at Sonke Gender Justice.

Her research interest lies in issues affecting black LGBTQIA+ women in South Africa; her Honours thesis was on creative approaches as dialogue for LGBTQIA+ Intimate Partner Violence. This thesis, Beyond the rainbow: creative approaches as dialogue for LGBTQIA+ intimate partner violence, was published in the Journal Of Contemporary African Studies.

Uvile is the co-founder of a multimedia production company, Thamba Creatives, which tells women's stories in South Africa. Her debut novel, Dreaming In Colour, does just that, telling the story of Langa, a young woman navigating relationships, self, and memory. It is Langa's story of coming out to herself, of discerning the history behind the closed door of conscious memory.

When it comes to her creativity, she prioritises interdisciplinary praxis and her stance is, "Why wait?" In another life, Uvile was a cat.

Obinna Obioma is a ghost, liberal, Virgo, tutor and literary gigolo. He's had his fair share of long-suffering getting his obsessions & agitation into Writers Space Africa, Active Muse, Jacana, Lunaris, K and L, Love Africa Press, Poets In Nigeria, Brittle Paper, Akuko Magazine & elsewhere. There are other cravings forthcoming, and he doesn't promise they'd be the last. He has myopia and wears an unmedicated glass to deceive his own bad sight. He tweets @ OOberyn or on any other media where his name and works pop up when you Google "Obinna Obioma Gigolo".

Moses Abukutsa is 38 years old. He writes poetry and fiction. He was shortlisted for the 2017 NALIF (Nyanza Literary Festival) literary prize for his short story Abraham's Cremation. He is also a member of WSA (Writers Space Africa), Kenya chapter. He has published short stories and poetry online with Kalahari Review, Praxis, African Writer, Kikwetu, Afritondo, Storymoja and khusoko. com, an East African Online Business platform. Abukutsa is a high school teacher of English and Literature and lives in Western Kenya.